TIME WILL TELL

A Witch in Time: Vee Book 3

STEPHANIE DAMORE

Chapter 1

Most nights, I don't dream. In fact, some nights, especially those after a particularly trying case, I do spell work before bedtime to ensure I don't. I'd like to think fate played a role as to why my shields were down that night. In one moment, there was only darkness. The next, there was Michael and his call for help.

"Vee! I need you!" His words rang in my head. I woke with my brow creased in concentration. I lay quietly, listening in the stillness and taking stock of my darkened bedroom. It was as messy as ever, but the room was silent. The seconds ticked by, with the rustling leaves being the only reply. I wondered if I truly had heard my boyfriend's voice. I couldn't even remember what he had said.

Wherever the voice had come from, no one was talking to me now. I rolled around to my side and tugged the comforter with me, preparing to settle in and try to fall back asleep. It was in that quiet space where I wasn't quite in dreamland but not fully awake when Michael's call for help rang out again.

"Vee, help." His voice was more of a whisper, a prayer, and not a shout.

My eyes snapped open.

"Michael?"

Again, there was silence, but somewhere, deep inside, I could feel his plea. I knew I hadn't imagined it, but the harder I focused on his words, the more he slipped away. I realized this wasn't a matter for consciousness. Michael was reaching out to me on a metaphysical level, and I had to reply likewise. Easier said than done when your heart was thumping painfully in your chest.

Astral projection was something that took years to perfect. When you used astral projection, your physical body remained unconscious in one spot while you projected yourself to another. It was only since I had begun working for the Agency of Paranormal Particularities that I had fully honed my skills, and it wasn't foolproof. The Great Big Unknown was a massive place, which was why I reserved the skill for emergencies, like when I needed to reach my Siamese cat familiar, Agatha. As my familiar, Agatha was the easiest for me to connect with, but Michael and I had also formed a bond. I could only hope that it was strong enough for me to follow.

"Magic, don't fail me now," I whispered before taking deep, calming breaths. I closed my eyes and tried to let go, knowing that was the only way for this to work. My magic uncoiled within me like muscle memory, bringing forth a swath of colors. Bubble gum pink and deep greens swirled on the back of my eyelids. I watched the bold scene unfold as the colors danced and more blended in. Vibrant red exploded like a firework, and lemony yellow squiggled past. A soft piano concerto played quietly in the background. It started as a single piano playing a simple tune until the music swelled and the full orchestra joined in. I allowed the music to move me. My lungs inhaled with the crescendo, and I pulled free from my body.

My spirit traveled through time and space, flying forward, searching for the blue wisps of Michael's magic. Over the last year and a half, I had come to know Michael's magical signature better than my own. I was always told that's what happened when you fell in love, but this was the first time I'd ever experienced it. If you thought the strength of our bond scared the heck out of me, you'd be right. But I didn't have time to dwell on my insecurities and what they meant for the future. Right now, I was just grateful I could trace Michael's cry for help.

I stopped moving and found myself suspended in space.

"Where are you?" I called out into the darkness. Eerie silence replied.

The thread of Michael's magic was a hair's breadth. Soon the trace would disappear entirely, and I'd be left swimming in a sea of emptiness.

One by one, the colors faded.

My body grew cold.

I knew the further I floated into the ether, the harder it would be to get back to my body.

As I stood there weightlessly, searching for some sign, a clue as to where Michael was, a vision began to play before me. I didn't know how Michael was doing it. It was magic I hadn't seen before. The images captivated me and had my pulse quickening and power pulsing. I recognized the setting. It was evening in New York City, 1964, which was the present day for Michael. I could identify the time period the second I spotted a car on the curb and the convenience store on the corner. It was Michael's neighborhood. He was there in the alley-way, and he wasn't alone. I gasped as I witnessed a large man throw Michael against the brick wall. He grunted as his body hit the ground. My magic burned hot and bright. Electricity filled my finger-tips, and I instinctively shot it forward, sending my power into the unknown. Nothing mattered. I was too far away. Another man kicked Michael in the stomach as he lay on his side. Michael wrapped his arms around his middle, protecting himself the best he could. I had no idea why he wasn't fighting back with magic, why he couldn't fight back. I needed to get to him and not through astral projection.

It was at the realization when I knew I had to get back to my body that Michael gave one last primitive cry. My name ripped from his lips and sent shivers down my spine. And then he passed out.

Michael's cry jolted me back to my body. I felt like someone had hit me with a stun gun in my chest. I woke with a start. My hands gripped the sheets. In the chaos, I'd tossed my comforter onto the floor along with my pillows. The bedding covered my discarded bell-bottomed jeans and button-up shirt from yesterday's nineteen seventy time jump. My heart hammered. I could feel the pressure pulsing through my veins. I had to consciously remind myself that I was here in the present and not with Michael. It was a bitter reality to accept. I'd failed him, but not for long. I needed to jump back to 1964 and find him. Now.

I tried to stand, to get my bearings, but my feet had become twisted in the sheets, creating a cotton binding. It was still dark out. The new moon only added to the blackness. A dim light in the hallway filtered in from the cracked bedroom door, but it wasn't enough light to help me break free.

I stumbled off the bed.

"Ugh!" I screamed in frustration. Finally, I loosened the sheets from my ankles and broke free. I had to go. I needed to get to Michael.

Agatha zoomed down the hallway. It was her nightly routine to wreak havoc around the farmhouse while I slept. She screeched to a halt outside my door.

Her head bopped the door open. "Wafs wong?" Her voice came out muffled. Agatha dropped the stuffed mouse out of her mouth and tried again, "What's wrong?"

I jammed my leg in a pair of jeans. "I have to go. I have to get to Michael. He's in trouble." The words flew out of my mouth.

"Where? What happened? Did you get a case?" Agatha looked around the room for a new case file. The Agency of Paranormal Particularities was known to assign cases any time, day or night. Often, they would magically appear out of thin air.

"No. Michael projected to me. He's in a fight." I struggled to say the words. The scene replayed in my head against my will. I shook my head to make it stop. "I can't explain it. I don't have time. I have to get to him." I darted across the room and yanked open my dresser for a pair of socks. "Where are my socks? Why can't I find any socks?" I growled in frustration as my hands scattered the shirts in my drawer. Why hadn't I turned on the light?

Agatha, showing so much composure that it was

annoying, evenly replied, "In the bottom drawer where they always are."

I wordlessly dropped to the bottom drawer.

"You need to calm down. You won't be able to help Michael out at all, acting frazzled the way you are," Agatha admonished me.

"I do not need a lecture right now!" My voice broke. I put my hands on my hips and took a steadying breath. I checked myself. "Sorry. You weren't there. You didn't see what I saw."

Agatha didn't miss a beat. "Regardless. If you want to help Michael, think with your head, not your heart."

I nodded. Agatha was right, even if I wasn't ready to admit it.

"Take a minute, change," Agatha motioned to my outfit with one of her tan-dipped paws. "Get your head in the game, and then go."

I looked down at my Prince T-shirt. The legendary musician was still a child in 1964. "You're right." I wasn't slowing down, though. I yanked off my clothes as quickly as I had put them on, switching out the T-shirt and jeans for black pedal pushers, a floral blouse, and a light pink, soft wool coat. Forget the coordinating hat and gloves. I didn't have time for it.

My cell phone rang on the bedside table, and I saw that it was my best friend and fellow time-traveling witch, Lexi Sanders. She no doubt felt my emotions ripple through the atmosphere. Lexi was gifted at picking up people's emotions like that.

"Will you answer that and fill her in? Tell her I'll call her when I can." I was proud of how much more even my voice sounded.

"Do you want me to come with you?"

I blinked at my familiar for a moment. She never offered to go with me anymore. Ever. She preferred staying home, napping on the back of the couch, and catching mice in the barn.

I swallowed nervously. "No, I got it. Thanks." Somehow having Agatha with me would only make things seem worse.

Chapter 2

I focused on the alleyway as I traveled through space. It was a risky move as anyone could see me pop into existence, but I was willing to chance it. Normally, I was more careful, reappearing in bathroom stalls or dressing rooms. But tonight, I blinked into existence right on the corner of West 10th and Hudson. I sprinted to the alleyway, directly across the street, and almost collided with the front of a yellow taxi. My hand smacked the hood, but it didn't slow me down. The cab driver yelled something, but his words didn't even register.

I already knew I was too late before I reached the alleyway. It was a gut feeling. The empty alleyway confirmed it. I turned my head back and forth, looking further down into the darkness. The only things I saw were metal trash cans and puddles of water. It was only then that I realized it was raining. It was only a sprinkle, but water and electricity don't mix. The electrical charge coming off my fingertips was strong enough to send a bolt of lightning into the atmosphere. I needed to regain control. I should find some comfort in the fact that Michael wasn't lying dead in the alleyway, but I didn't.

My instincts told me to stay on alert.

I swallowed nervously and took one last look around. Residual magic hung in the air. I could feel it. I focused with my sixth sense and picked up the wisps of Michael's magic. I was wrong, he had used it, but he'd been outnumbered. The loamy scent of shifter condensed like clouds in the small space, competing with the petrichor from the falling rain. Shifters were strong, and if they'd snuck up on Michael, I could see why he went down. The question was, where was he now?

I felt like I could stand there all night, and I'd never have the answers I needed. I decided to walk the short distance to Michael's. With any luck, he was home nursing his wounds, and together we'd catch whoever did this to him.

It was only then, when I turned around, that I spotted an older man standing in the middle of the sidewalk. He had on a brown tweed coat and matching hat. A grocery bag sat forgotten on the ground. An apple had fallen out and rolled a foot away. The man stood slack-jawed. His eyes were unblinking as he stared at me.

"Shoot," I hissed under my breath. The man must've witnessed my arrival. I shook my head and jogged across the street toward him. The man snapped out of it as I approached, seeming startled when I headed right for him.

I stopped when we were only inches apart.

"Hi, sorry, didn't mean to startle you. Have you been standing here long?" I tried to be as friendly and engaging as possible despite the fact that I had just given this man the shock of his life.

"I–I–I," the man mumbled the syllable repeatedly.

"Did you, by chance, see what happened across the street? I'm worried about a friend."

"They–they–they," the man pointed to the alleyway.

"There was someone that was just there."

The man looked at me with wide eyes nervously. "They left," he managed to get out.

"Did you see which way they went?" I was back to scanning the area for Michael.

"There was smoke. Blue smoke. Then you--"

I interrupted the man. "Blue smoke?"

"A whole bunch of it, blowing 'round."

It was my turn to be speechless. I mentally sifted through all the spells I knew but came up empty.

"Then they disappeared," the man finished. He

looked down at the sidewalk and blinked his eyes into focus. When he looked up, his thoughts seemed clearer. "Then you appeared." The man looked at me as if seeing me truly for the first time. "They disappeared, and then you appeared." He said again with stronger conviction.

"The men in the alley disappeared?" I wanted to make sure I understood the gentleman correctly. I didn't bother repeating the part about me suddenly appearing.

The man looked at me and nodded solemnly.

The nervous knot in my stomach tightened. I thought Michael might have time-jumped when the man said they disappeared, but the blue smoke had me second-guessing that assumption. As far as I knew, and I knew a fair amount about time travel, it never resulted in smoke aftereffects, which meant some other form of transportation spell was at play. The question was, what was the spell, and who did it belong to?

It was pointless to ask the gentleman any more questions. He wouldn't have the answers. The best thing I could do now was offer him some peace.

I was thankful that it was springtime and that the man's hands were bare and not tucked away in gloves. I reached out and gently squeezed his hand. I had to be careful, with how hot my magic was burning, I was likely to erase more of this man's memory than the last ten minutes.

I took a calming breath. It was more for my sake than for his. I sent a small pulse of electricity from my fingertips up the man's arm until it reached his brain and rewired his memory.

I calmly let go and waited for the man's consciousness to float back down to earth.

"So, I just need to turn left, and the pharmacy is right up the street?"

The man nodded numbly.

"Oh here, you dropped this." I bent down and picked up the man's grocery bag and wayward apple. "Sorry for bumping into you like that. I need to watch where I'm going."

The man continued to blink at me.

"Thank you so much for the directions. I hope you can head home now and enjoy your evening." I patted the man on his arm and smiled softly.

"You too," the man mumbled. He paused on the sidewalk momentarily before turning and heading in the opposite direction.

I wasted no time heading to Michael's. On the outside, I looked cool and composed. On the inside, I was a complete wreck. My heart hadn't stopped beating erratically since Michael's voice called to me, and my breathing was just as uneven.

I could only hope my boyfriend had disappeared of his own free will. With any luck, he'd be waiting for me at his apartment. But even as I thought the words, I doubted they were true.

MICHAEL LIVED in a very utilitarian space. You either had a bedroom or a living room, depending on if the hide-a-bed was pulled down or not. I didn't have a key to Michael's place, not because he didn't want me to have one. A secret smile played across my lips when he offered, and I told him it wasn't necessary. Locks were my specialty. All I had to do was grip the handle and imagine inserting a key into the slot. As the tumblers aligned, I'd turn the invisible key in my head and release the latch.

I did the same now. The lock clicked open. I twisted my wrist, and the black wood door swung inward.

The instant I stepped across the threshold, the scent of shifter hit me. It was even more potent than the alleyway. There was no mistaking it. A shifter or, more likely, a group of shifters by the strength of their lingering scent, had been inside Michael's apartment. I took a step back in case they were still inside.

Michael's apartment was the shape of a shoebox and about the same size. The kitchen, living room, and bedroom shared the same space. A closet-sized bathroom was hidden behind a curtain. A small coat closet was the only other door. I stood on the offense as I swept Michael's room with my eyes. Then, I walked across the room quietly, reaching the bathroom and tossing the curtain back, ready to strike, but the space was empty. I was alone.

I swallowed the lump down in my throat.

I hadn't thought Michael would be here, but that didn't mean the realization didn't hurt.

I continued to search Michael's apartment, looking for a clue. The space was tidy without one of his case files in sight, not that he had a kitchen table to leave documents out on. A single bowl and spoon sat drying on the rack next to the sink, taking up the kitchen's only counter space.

Michael wasn't a neat freak. It was more of a testament to how much he wasn't home. Both Michal and I were the job. He as a detective for the NYPD and me as an agent. If it weren't for each other, we wouldn't have a social life. Surprisingly, I was good with that. Life with Michael was comfortable. I was happy. Those simple thoughts caused a single tear to slip out of the corner of my eye and leave a trail down my cheek. I used the back of my hand to wipe it away.

If only I could go to the police department for help or even find out what case Michael was working. It probably wasn't related, and as far as the NYPD was concerned, Michael was a regular detective, but you never knew. It wouldn't be the first time Michael's job led him on a paranormal chase. It was a testament to how many supernaturals called the Big Apple home. It wasn't like Michael worked for the Agency of Paranormal Particularities, but still, he arrested his fair share of supernaturals, and this was clearly an unorthodox case.

I turned toward his dresser. I hesitated. It felt like a violation of Michael's privacy to rummage through his things, but what choice did I have?

I slowly slid the first drawer open. Inside, underneath a pile of shirts, was a gold pocket watch, a couple of black and white photographs, and a handful of tens and twenties. I counted the cash. It was just over two hundred dollars. I pocketed forty with a mental promise to Michael that I'd pay it back as soon as I had access to my own funds. I skimmed through the photos, recognizing Michael as a young boy along with his sister, Karen. I assumed the two adults in the photo were his parents; I didn't know them. They had died in a car accident when Michael was a teenager. His grandmother, Edith, had finished raising them.

My hand reached out for the gold pocket watch. I closed my eyes and opened my senses, hoping to pick up Michael's energy, but instead, I found someone else's. The threads were a faint green. I twisted my lips in thought. The watch most likely belonged to Michael's father or grandfather even. I had hoped to use it to help me scry for Michael, but it wouldn't be much use to me if his energy wasn't attached to it. Scrying spells worked best when you had something that belonged to the person you were tracking to focus on. The more important the object was to the person, the more energy they imprinted upon it, and the easier it was to find them. It was even better if the object was made from metal. Metal was always a better conductor for energy.

I continued to search the rest of Michael's drawers, but I wasn't finding anything I could use. I stood up, feeling defeated. With my hands on my hips, I surveyed the room.

"What can I use?" I was about to throw out a spell to help me locate an object when I spotted something achingly familiar on the counter next to Michael's phone.

I stepped closer to prove my eyes weren't deceiving me.

They weren't.

My hand shook as I picked up the leather flip case and opened it up.

It was Michael's badge.

I held the badge to my heart and walked steadily to the bathroom. Witches can scry in a couple of different ways. One way required a crystal like a quartz along with a map. The crystal acted like a pendulum, swaying until it dropped on the object's location. Unfortunately, I didn't have a crystal or a map on me. The other required a smooth surface like a mirror or a body of water that you can peer into like a looking glass. This was the method I planned to try.

Michael's bathroom mirror wasn't expansive by any stretch of the imagination. It was more like one foot by two feet in area. But it was clear, and the room was full of his energy. I was betting on those facts, plus the badge, to aid me.

I took deep breaths, inhaling through my nose, filling my lungs, and slowly exhaling out my mouth. I tried to blow away the stress and anxiety from the past couple of hours and focus on the present.

I relaxed my body and focused on the threads of energy that were bound to the badge. I waited in silence, calming my mind and soul. When I felt ready, I spoke the following words:

Power I need, come to me.

With harm to none, so mote it be.

Michael's energy pulsed around the badge. I looked down at the emblem in my hand and focused my intention onto it:

Show me Michael here and now

So I may save him

Free from sorrow

Safe at last

Undo the past

And set him free

As I will it, so mote it be.

I gripped the edge of the porcelain sink with my free hand and leaned forward to look into the mirror. A faded image flickered in the reflection. But it was dim, and I could barely make out Michael's features. I wouldn't have even known it was him if I hadn't specifically requested the spell to look for him.

I needed to strengthen the spell. I tried again. I took a deep breath and closed my eyes. On the exhale, I said:

Sharpen the image, make it more clear

Show me Michael Cooper, the detective I hold dear.

I waited a moment and then fluttered my eyes open and stared into the mirror. My brow creased in concentration as I fought to bring Michael into focus. It was easy to see my reflection, but Michael's was still fuzzy.

"Please, let me see." My breath was a mere whisper. I held my gaze in the mirror, waiting, hoping. I was no longer breathing. I needed something to work with. Some lead to chase. Anything.

The Universe answered my prayers.

For a split second, I saw Michael clearly. His eyes were closed, and he was sitting on the floor. I couldn't tell if his hands were tied behind his back or not. There wasn't enough time. The image was brief. No matter how hard I concentrated or pleaded with the Universe, I couldn't bring the picture back. I knew a failed spell when I saw one. I exhaled and pushed off the sink, returning to an upright position.

I breathed out a sigh of frustration. What if I didn't find him? What if I was already too late? The what ifs spun uncontrollably through my head. The thoughts were making me dizzy with worry.

It was getting out of hand.

I couldn't think about what would happen if I never found Michael, or worse, found him dead. I couldn't let my mind go there.

I needed to think like a detective and not an emotionally invested girlfriend.

How many times had I already reminded myself what needed to be done? Too many.

It was time to get to work. There was only one place where I knew to go.

The billiard hall was shifter headquarters. Well, not so much the billiard hall as the illegal gambling den in its basement. I wasn't sure how welcoming they'd be since the last time we'd parted, it hadn't been on the best of terms, but I had to try. The shifter scent was the strongest lead I had.

Chapter 3

After taking one last look around the apartment, I locked up after myself and headed for the subway. There was a time when public transportation made me nervous, mostly because I wasn't familiar with all the stops, and I was always afraid I would miss mine. But not anymore. I rode the rail north to East Harlem where the billiard hall was located.

I knew what to expect before reaching the top step. Mixed in with the graffitied walls and littered trash was the scent of shifter. It hung in the air and seeped into the concrete. This was their domain. I was the trespasser. My powers hummed across my body and crackled at my fingertips. I welcomed the surge. I was ready for whatever would happen.

I had to be.

As I cleared the last step, I instinctively looked up at the sky to identify the moon's phase. It was officially nighttime. I had no idea what time precisely as I hadn't bothered to look at a clock at Michael's. Nor did I know what day of the week it was. All I knew was that when I time jumped, it had been twilight, and now the sky was bathed in ink. The darkness matched my mood. And if I were mistaken, which I rarely was when it came to the moon, it would be a full moon in the next day or two. Shifters always had to change on the full moon. It's just the way they were wired. Great, just what I needed, shifters at their peak power.

I walked directly to the billiard hall. A neon open sign flickered in the window, with the blown glass barely illuminating the end. I stepped around the glass beer bottles scattered along the sidewalk, along with the discarded cigarette butts and chip wrappers, and yanked open the green security door.

The place was empty.

I hadn't expected that.

I stumbled on the threshold, wondering if I should still go in. Looking around the hall, it looked like whatever had caused the bar to close had happened suddenly. Patrons had abandoned their drinks. A mixture of half-full martini glasses, tumblers, and beer bottles cluttered the tabletops. As I stepped closer, a chill ran through my body. The drinks still had ice in them. Whatever had happened here had happened tonight.

I continued to survey the scene.

Chairs were toppled onto the floor. A wayward cigar gave off tendrils of sweet-smelling smoke. Players had abandoned the billiard tables mid-game. Striped and solid balls lay scattered across the green felt with cues dropped on the floor like sticks.

I absently rubbed my hands across my shoulders to warm myself up. It was then that I realized it wasn't the energy giving me chills but the actual temperature. The billiard hall was freezing. Perhaps the building was always kept cool, and all the people inside only made it feel warm, but this seemed extreme, especially with the mild temperatures outside.

I quit thinking about the temperature the moment I eyed the stairwell to the gaming den. I wondered what clues I'd find in the basement.

I kept a watchful eye as I made my way toward the stairs. I was a smart witch. A brave witch. A powerful which. And a witch who'd be lying if she said she wasn't nervous as she made her way slowly down the steps.

I knew what I should find downstairs. There should be scattered round tables with poker chips, coins, and dollar bills tossed into the center. I should see playing cards, more cocktails, and shifters huddled around the tables, throwing out their best bets. There should be a steady roar of voices as gamblers cheered and leered over their wins and losses.

Instead, my foot almost slipped on the bottom step when it made contact with the ice. I hung onto the handrail and ducked low to go under the icicles forming from the doorframe.

It took a lot to shock me, and at that moment, I was speechless. The entire den, including a handful of shifters, was frozen solid. Everything sparkled in enchanted blue ice. I didn't bother going any further. No one here could speak, and I didn't dare touch the ice with my bare hands. Magic could be sneaky like that. I wasn't about to be cursed.

I backed up slowly. This case had suddenly turned into something much larger than my missing boyfriend and a pack of rogue shifters. I shivered, this time because of the magic, and found myself backtracking upstairs to put the frozen scene behind me.

I didn't quit moving until I swung back out the hall's metal door, and the warm spring air washed over me. It was only about sixty degrees out, but compared to the Arctic basement, it felt like summertime in July, even with the musky scent of shifter in the air.

"She's a witch!" A young boy said to his friend.

Out of the corner of my eye, I saw a trio of young boys make a run for it. Ironically, I knew who they were from working on a previous case.

I didn't even hesitate as I sprinted after them. They were young, and they were fast, but I was determined. That trio of boys knew something, and I was desperate to find out what.

"Stop!" I huffed as they rounded the corner, and I kicked up the pace to try to close the distance. "I need your help!" The boys didn't slow down. "I'll pay you twenty bucks!"

The boys screeched to a stop.

"Sorry, Michael," I mumbled under my breath.

"Show us the money," the first boy said, raising his chin. I think if I remember correctly, his name was Rico.

"Right here." I reached into my purse and retrieved a twenty. I waved the bill in front of me. I probably could've gotten them to stop for a lot less, but once the figure slipped past my lips, I wasn't about to take it back. Twenty bucks was well worth over a hundred dollars currently.

"Don't listen to her, Rico. She's a cop. Don't you remember?" The second boy, I never did catch his name, said.

"I'm not a cop. My friend, Detective Cooper, is, but I'm not. Promise." I tried to look as innocent as possible.

"We don't want no trouble," the youngest boy of the group spoke up. His voice shook from nerves.

"I don't want any trouble either. I'm just trying to find out what happened over there."

"Why don't you ask your friends? You're one of them." Rico held out his hands for the cash. I reluctantly put the bill in his hand. I guess it would be up to them to fight it out to see who got what.

"I don't have anything to do with what happened down there. I'm looking for my friend, the detective you know. Someone beat him up real bad, and now he's missing. I have to find him." The group of boys looked at one another. I didn't have to fake the emotion that played out across my face. I was worried sick about Michael. You could read it plain as day on my features, from how my lip trembled to the tears that threatened to spill out of my eyes.

"Man, now you going to make her cry," the second boy said. Rico looked at his buddies as if telling them to be quiet. Rico leaned in closer to me. I followed suit and took another step toward him. "There's a really bad warlock in town. He's threatening all the shifters. You don't do what he says," Rico looked to either side of him warily. "He freezes you."

I wrinkled my brow in concentration. "What is he trying to make the shifters do?" The group of boys took a step back. It was clear they weren't going to give up any more information.

"Look, we gotta go." The second boy tugged Rico's shirtsleeve.

"Our mamas are going to be worried about us," the smallest boy of the trio piped in.

"Why you gotta bring up our mamas?" Rico asked, looking embarrassed.

"Thanks for the info. You boys stay safe."

"I don't know what you're talking about. We didn't tell you nothing," Rico kicked the pebble in front of his shoe and turned and walked away. I watched the group until they disappeared around the corner, and then I did the same, turning around and heading back to the subway. But even as I walked away, I couldn't help but feel like eyes were on the back of my neck. Someone or something was watching me.

Chapter 4

I felt more in control when I got back to Michael's. On the subway ride back to Midtown, I came up with a plan. The alpha shifter was the equivalent of a mafia godfather in all ways, and it just so happened that I knew a Godfather. Michael's close friend, Jim Wilson, married Mary Rigatti, whose father was the alpha of the Chicago shifters. As a lion shifter, Mr. Rigatti was the king of the urban jungle. After I saved his daughter's wedding (and life, I might add), the man told me I was a "friend of the family." I still wasn't sure what that entailed, but hopefully, it meant that he would tell me what was going on in New York City.

The only thing was, I had to find Michael's address book. I'd seen him reference it on more than one occasion. It was a small black leather book about three by five inches in dimension. His initials were carved on the cover in silver lettering. I could only hope the book was in the apartment somewhere and not at his office. I wasn't sure where else to look, given that I had already searched his dresser. I suppose it could be in a kitchen drawer or maybe a coat pocket. It wasn't like looking for a needle in a haystack, but the bottom line was that it would be much easier to form a quick spell to locate the book.

The scent of shifter wasn't surprising when I unlocked the front door and stepped inside. It didn't mean it was pleasant, just that it was expected.

I shrugged off my coat and laid it across Michael's bed. Then, I stood in the middle of the room and closed my eyes, taking a calming breath. I pictured the address book right down to the gilded edges and carved initials. The closer I visualized the image, the easier it would be to track.

After feeling calm and centered, I said the magical words:

MAGIC COME TO ME.
Help me find what I cannot see.
I beseech thee to lead me to the book
for in it lie the answers I seek

<u>That may set Michael free.</u>
<u>As I will it, so mote it be.</u>

I FLUTTERED my eyes open and waited for the spell to take effect. I had been facing the kitchen, thinking that was the way my intuition would lead me, but instead found myself turning and walking toward the front door. I gave an inward groan. I didn't want to have to walk to Michael's precinct and try to explain why I needed the address book. I could always bewitch whoever came across my path, but it would've been easier to find the address book in his apartment. Which was why I was pleasantly surprised when my feet bypassed the front door and stopped in front of the coat closet.

I smiled as an outward thanks of gratitude. Michael must've left his address book in a coat pocket. I eagerly gripped the closet handle and swung open the door, and that was when a dead body fell out.

"Ack!" I jumped aside just in the nick of time. The body hit the floor with a dull thud. I swallowed uncomfortably as a dozen questions raced through my head. If I thought the smell of shifter was strong before, it was nothing compared to the scent now polluting Michael's apartment. If he had a window, I would've opened it immediately. I was speechless.

Why was a dead shifter in Michael's closet? Did this mean Michael killed him? And why shove the man in the closet? Did Michael have something to do with the frozen basement at the billiard hall? It would explain why the shifters wanted revenge and had jumped him in the alleyway. But Michael wouldn't have attacked someone unprovoked, and he certainly didn't make it a habit of killing anyone. I needed a moment to think, but the proximity to the dead body made it hard for me to get a rational thought to filter through my brain.

I shuffled back to the kitchen until the top of my hip bumped into the countertop. I needed help, that much was clear, and there was only one person I could think to reach out to.

I was going to have to astral project and reach out to Agatha. I wasn't looking forward to it, and I had no idea if I would be strong enough to do it. Astral projecting and time jumping left me physically and spiritually drained. My powers had grown in the last year, but even I had my limits. It was foolish of me to push them, but I wasn't sure what else to do. You know what they say, desperate times call for desperate measures. The only problem was, I wasn't about to lie down and get cozy in the middle of Michael's bed with a dead man on the floor. I needed somewhere safe to let go and reach out to Agatha.

I was debating where that could be. The only

answer I came up with was a hotel room. I was getting ready to take a little bit more of Michael's cash again and head out when a knock on the front door stopped me dead in my tracks.

I looked to the left and the right. There was no way I could put the dead man back in the closet. I suppose I could lift the bed, drag the man to the center of the floor, and then pull the bed back down to cover him, but even that would take time. Better yet, why would I even answer the door? See what I mean about rational thoughts being in short supply? I would wait the visitor out. It should only take a minute or two. People never waited outside doors for too long.

It was a shame Michael's apartment door didn't have a peephole. If it had, you could bet I would look outside, but until he had one installed, I would never know who the visitor was.

Or so I thought.

There was another knock followed by a man's voice. "Vee? I know you're in there. Open up. It's Deacon."

I FROZE. I only knew one Deacon, and he worked for the Agency. Deacon wasn't an agent, though, but a case manager. His job was to gather the data, create a cover, and send us witches back in time.

I took a steadying breath. I had no reason not to trust Deacon, except that there was a dead shifter on the floor, and I had no idea how he got there.

Regardless, Deacon knew I was in here, and there was only one way out of the apartment. Not only that, I was curious about what he was doing here and how he knew I was inside.

I called my powers forth in case I ended up needing them to defend myself. Warmth started in my belly and extended to my limbs with every measured heartbeat.

Deacon knocked again, and I replied by swinging open the door. The man tripped forward. It seemed he had been listening at the door, and he hadn't expected me to answer it. The chagrined expression and flushed cheeks confirmed my suspicions.

But the blood quickly drained from his face. "There's a dead body on the floor." He pointed at the shifter.

"Uh-huh." I motioned for Deacon to come into the room the rest of the way and shut the door behind him.

"Why is there a dead body on the floor? You time jumped, what, two hours ago, and you already killed someone?"

"I didn't kill anyone, and how do you know how long I've been here?" Deacon looked even more uncomfortable, if that was even possible. "Since when has the Agency started keeping tabs on me when I'm not working a case?"

Deacon avoided my gaze.

I stepped into his line of sight. "You better start talking."

"I don't know anything, I swear. Well, not much anyway. I mean, I don't make those decisions. You know that. I'm just a peon like you."

"You're going to have to do better than that." I snapped my fingers, and a spark flicked in the air.

Deacon swallowed uncomfortably. "Listen, I don't know everything that's going on here, but what I do know is that it's much bigger than you and I. If I were you? I'd walk away."

I looked at my colleague as if he had lost his mind. "Walk away? What in the heck are you talking about? My boyfriend is missing, and there's a dead shifter in his apartment. You're insane if you think I'm walking away."

"It's not your business, Vee."

"Excuse me?" I was seeing red, or make that electric blue. Deacon would be lucky if I didn't blast him back to the future.

The man sensed he was in trouble as he began to backtrack. "What I mean is that Michael's working the case. Not you."

I cut Deacon off. "What do you mean Michael's working the case? Since when does he work for the Agency?"

Deacon coughed. "Er. I'm not at liberty to discuss the details."

"Not at liberty?" I grounded out. I wanted to ask what was with the Agency and all the secrets lately, but if I was honest, the Agency always operated under secrecy. It was the fact that Michael had kept his involvement from me that I couldn't get over. The two of us didn't have secrets, or so I thought. I felt defeated. "Why didn't the Agency ask me? I'm here enough." I motioned to the apartment, unable to keep the hurt out of my voice.

Deacon shrugged. "Conflict of interest."

I wanted to pull my hair out. "Deacon! You're talking in circles. Give me something to work with here."

"You need to walk away, Vee. I'm telling you. It's too risky. The Agency isn't willing to risk any more agents."

"You can't abandon him!" I was shouting at this point, and I didn't care.

"This is out of my hands."

"I'm not leaving. I will jump back week after week, as long as it takes until I find Michael and figure out what is happening here."

"Vee," Deacon closed his eyes. I could tell he was frustrated, and maybe there was a hint of desperation in his voice, but I didn't care. It paled in comparison to how I felt about losing Michael.

"Don't Vee me. You either tell me what's going on, or you lose me as an agent forever."

Deacon sighed. It was a deep, weary expression.

"Can't you tell me anything?"

Deacon closed his eyes. I gave him a moment. When he opened them again, I looked at him with raised eyebrows, expecting answers, or at the very least, a promise of action. "Let me talk to the boss and see what they say. I don't think they'll go for it, though, but I'll try. We've already lost too many agents."

"Who else have we lost?" My voice trembled. It had been years since an agent went missing in the field. Of course, it happens from time to time. I knew all too well the risk of the job before I even signed on. My mother worked for the Agency before I did, and she never came home.

But my question was going to go unanswered. "I'm sorry, Vee, but--"

"You're not at liberty to discuss it." I finished Deacon's sentence for him.

"I'm going to call the cleanup crew and have them come and take care of the shifter. I don't think you should stay here, regardless of your plans," Deacon quickly added when I opened my mouth to protest. I wasn't about to leave the city. But even I had to admit that Deacon was probably right. I was going to have to set up a home base someplace else. The question was where.

"The agency has a standard room at the Fitzger-ald." It was Deacon's turn to sound defeated. "I'll go make a call and tell them you're on your way."

Chapter 5

The Fitzgerald was a five-star hotel located in midtown. I didn't care what the star rating was or where the hotel was situated as long as it had a phone line. I could make anything work. Luckily, my reasoning came back to me before I left Michael's, and I managed to lift his address book out of a trench coat hanging in the closet. Maybe it was out of guilt, or perhaps he was being kind, but Deacon arranged to have a cab waiting for me out front.

"I'll be in touch," he said as I folded myself into the back seat and Deacon shut the door. He leaned through the front passenger side window and passed a couple of dollars to the driver. I nodded my thanks. I had plenty of cash to pay for the cab, but I had a feeling Deacon was trying to make amends. I knew he was only doing his job, and I couldn't blame him for the feelings swirling around in my tummy. The uneasiness weighed heavily like I'd swallowed a block of ice that wouldn't budge. I felt numb with the cold. You couldn't find out that your boyfriend was working as a secret agent and not feel out of sorts. I wondered how many cases he had taken on for the agency and why he hadn't confided in me. I tried to remind myself that I had kept a case from Michael before, and at the time, I felt that I had a good reason for doing so. I tried to extend the same grace to Michael even though it wasn't in my nature to do so.

I checked into the hotel in a daze. The opulence of the lobby with its dark green carpet, crystal chandeliers, and gold accents blurred in the background, like the dozens of people mingling about. The lobby shared the space with the hotel's bar. Laughter spilled out, and I closed my eyes to tune the noise out. The quicker I could get into my room, the better.

I rode the elevator to the tenth floor and was relieved to be greeted with silence. Once tucked safely inside my room, with the *Do Not Disturb* sign placed on the door, I finally had a chance to look at a clock. It was after ten at night. Propriety dictated that I wait until morning to call Jim, but time wasn't on my side, and manners could be forgiven. Thankfully, Chicago was on central time, meaning it was an hour earlier there.

I quickly found Jim's number filed in the W

section of Michael's address book. Focusing, I used the rotary phone to crank out the area code and the phone number. I sat on the edge of the bed before standing again and waiting for the lines to connect. After three rings, I convinced myself to sit down once more and try to be patient.

"Hello?" A woman's voice answered. I recognized it right away. This was even better than reaching Jim.

"Mary? It's Vee Harper."

"Vee, my goodness, it's so good to hear from you. Although maybe I shouldn't say that. You are calling awfully late."

I was back to standing again. Thank goodness the phone had a decent length cord as I began to pace in front of the nightstand. "I know, and I'm sorry about that. Something bad has happened, and I need your help." I swallowed back the emotions that I felt bubbling up in my chest. It was hard to say the words, but Mary was patient.

"It's Michael, isn't it?" She guessed at my silence.

I nodded even though she couldn't see me. "It is. He was working a case, and a couple of guys jumped him in an alleyway. I think they were shifters." I didn't need to say more. Mary knew all about the strength shifters could wield. I took a steadying breath. "There's more, but I'm hoping your father can help me."

Mary gasped. "Is it that bad?"

"It's probably worse. Whatever's happening here in New York City is big." I thought of the frozen gambling den and the young boys' fears. "I think it's affecting the whole shifter community, and if anyone would know --"

"It would be Papa," Mary finished my thoughts. "Let me get a hold of him. Are you staying at Michael's?"

"Not right now. I'm at the Fitzgerald." I left it at that. Mary didn't pry, and I was thankful.

"Give me a few minutes, and I'll see what I can do."

"Thank you." I hung up the phone and began pacing the room in earnest, wondering what Mr. Rigatti would say. I started to doubt he remembered me. It had been a hectic weekend, and people always say things in the rush of the moment. Maybe being a friend of the family meant I was invited over for summer barbecues, and not privy to shifter secrets. What if I offended the Alpha? I didn't want to be on his bad side.

Shockingly, the hotel room's phone rang two minutes later. I jumped in surprise and quickly regained my composure. "This is Vee," I said in the most professional voice I could muster.

"Ms. Harper, what can I do for you?" Mr. Rigatti's accented Italian voice purred through the line.

I kept it all business. "I'm hoping you can help me find Michael. A group of shifters jumped him in an alleyway, and then they disappeared. I mean that literally," I added in case Mr. Rigatti thought that I meant that I simply couldn't find him. "When I went to the billiard hall, the basement was encased in ice. A couple of shifters didn't get away." I left out the part about finding a dead body in Michael's closet.

Mr. Rigatti was silent for a moment. I started to doubt again if he would help me at all.

"Please, I need to find him. Don't tell me to walk away." I tried to keep the desperation out of my voice.

Again, there was more silence until the alpha finally spoke. "Here's what I'm going to do. I'll tell you what's going on in New York, but you have to promise you'll come to Chicago if the trouble blows this way. My pack doesn't need New York's problems."

"Absolutely." It seemed like an easy promise to keep. I waited patiently for Mr. Rigatti to continue.

"Good, because you've got a big problem."

"What's going on?"

"The way I hear it, a dark warlock is rounding up witches around the city. Don't go asking me his name because I don't know it, and I don't want to know it. All I know is the more powerful the witch, the more money he'll pay. If the shifters don't comply, they become the enemy."

"New York shifters became the enemy."

"Sounds like it."

"Any idea where this dark warlock is taking people?"

"Not a clue. But if I hear anything, I'll pass it on to Mary. I meant what I said, you're a friend of the family. We'll do what we can to help."

I clicked off with Mr. Rigatti and felt weary down to my bones. The adrenaline rush from being woken in the middle of the night and everything that followed had slowly worn away, leaving me drained with nothing but worry remaining. I decided there wasn't much I could do tonight. My powers were pretty much useless until I recharged a bit. Even if I got a couple of hours rest, it would be enough to help me reset and clear my mind. I didn't think I'd be able to fall asleep, but my body proved me wrong. Within a few moments of forcing myself to lie still, I fell into a dark, dreamless sleep.

Chapter 6

I woke the next day on a mission. I needed to talk to Michael's grandmother, Edith. The kind woman had helped us out on a previous case. Edith was a seer. She lived with his sister, Karen, in Pennsylvania along with her husband and a pack of children.

I could have called, but I felt this was a conversation best to be had in person. Not only that, but it was also almost impossible to get a word in over the phone when the kids were running around.

I made a quick stop back at Michael's apartment to retrieve his car keys. I don't know why I didn't think about taking it sooner. Again, I hadn't been thinking clearly. The apartment looked and smelled like new. The agency's cleaning crew had done a fantastic job ridding the apartment of shifter. I had no clue what scent spell they used, but it would be helpful to find out.

After leaving Michael's, I stopped by the gas station on the way out of town for the necessities, which included a custard doughnut, a cup of coffee, and a newspaper. I found out today was May 10, 1964. It was a Tuesday, which meant yesterday was Monday. I had never liked Mondays.

Two hours later, Michael's car bumped down the country road as I finished the drive to his sister's house. In many ways, seeing the farmhouse and the country scenery made me feel like I was coming home. If I didn't pass another car, I wouldn't have been able to tell the difference in the year. Country life could be timeless. Unfortunately, Michael didn't share the love of the country with me. He was a city boy, and I was a country girl. I found the country soothed me. It helped me regain my balance after fighting crime and kicking butt. New York City was too much. After visiting Michael, I had to escape all the city lights and the sheer number of people. I craved solitude. Michael thrived in chaos. Yet another reason why our time-traveling relationship worked well for us.

Gravel crunched under the car's tires as I bumped my way up the driveway. A border collie and a yellow lab came up from the backyard and barked to signal my arrival. Other than that, the house seemed quiet, which was odd. I stepped out of Michael's car and took a moment to steady myself. The dogs wagged their tails and sniffed my pants. I bent down to give them pats and buy myself a moment. I realized that I was nervous. I hated breaking bad news, especially to loved ones. Honestly, I wouldn't have told Karen what was going on if I didn't think she could somehow help. Karen had powers like the rest of Michael's family.

Michael's sister stepped out on the porch. She wore a white apron over a dark green day dress. I glanced up at her while continuing to give the dogs some love.

"No," Karen said, reading my expression and shaking her head. She closed her eyes and held onto the porch's wooden rail. I guess my expression wasn't as stoic as I'd hoped it was. Karen's husband was a police officer in Philly. She knew all about the risks that came with wearing a badge. I could only imagine the horrors that were going through her head.

I took a calming breath and stepped away from the pups. "He's not dead," I called out. "At least I don't think he is," I added in a quieter voice. Karen's eyes locked with mine, and I could see that she was already crying. "Is your grandmother here?"

Karen nodded and then held open the door for me to follow her. The farmhouse was a similar layout to my own. The living room was in the front. The kitchen was in the back. And a stairway ran up the middle, opening to a handful of bedrooms upstairs.

"Coffee?" Karen's voice shook.

"Please," I wasn't sure I could drink it, but it would give Karen something to do.

"My grandmother's out back reading. I'll be back in just a moment."

I nodded in understanding. Karen slipped out the back door, and I sat at the kitchen table. It was an odd feeling. The house was so quiet I could hear the grandfather clock in the living room ticking. I didn't know this house could be so still. I had been here on summer days and holidays. It was always filled with laughter, kids shrieking, and dogs barking. Never on a regular weekday during the school year. The lack of life was disconcerting. It made the gravity of the situation seem so much heavier.

"Vee? Where's Michael? What's going on?" Edith asked.

"That's what I'm hoping you can help me with," I said to the wise older woman. We sat together at the kitchen table, including Karen. The promise of coffee was forgotten.

The ladies looked at me expectantly. I wasn't sure if or how I could sugarcoat it. My throat suddenly felt parched.

"Go on, tell us what happened," Edith encouraged.

I nodded and swallowed uncomfortably. "Michael's gone missing." The grandmother and daughter shared a look. I plowed forward. "Monday night, he projected to me, asking for help." I took a steadying breath. "He woke me from my sleep. He was jumped in the alley by his house. By the time I could get to him, I was too late. He was gone."

"What do you mean gone? Did he time jump?" Karen asked.

"I don't think so. I found a witness, a regular human, and he mentioned seeing blue smoke."

"Blue smoke?" Karen looked at her grandmother once more.

I nodded. "The man said after they disappeared, all he saw was blue smoke. Does that sound familiar to either one of you?"

Edith looked thoughtful. "Some spells use smoke, but, gosh, it's been so long. I have to think about it." Her eyebrows bunched in concentration.

Edith's eyes got that far away look. Even though her gaze lined up with the empty chair beside me, I knew she saw something entirely different. Edith was doing what I was going to ask her to do without even asking. Her mind seemed to check out of our current surroundings as she attempted to track down Michael. Karen and I didn't say a word for fear of interrupting the process. The only movement Edith gave was a twitch of her eye or the tilt of her head. Occasionally, she would wrinkle her brow and lean forward as if trying to get a closer look. The minutes ticked by, and it grew more difficult to remain patient. I was dying to know what Edith was seeing.

"He's there." Edith squinted her eyes shut in concentration. "He's alive," she clarified. "I can't say that he's well. Our connection isn't strong enough." Edith again fell silent, and Karen and I were left waiting for more clues.

The grandfather clock counted the seconds, and I tried to look anywhere but at Edith. The emotions playing across her face were too much to bear.

Finally, Edith's eyes popped open, and she gasped, pulling my attention to her. Anguish poured forth from her watery blue eyes. "I'm sorry, I just can't. I'm not as strong as I used to be!" The woman's hands trembled as the tears fell down her cheeks.

"It's okay," Karen moved quickly, reaching over, and rubbing her grandmother's shoulder affectionately in a half-embrace.

"I'm sorry. I never meant to upset you." I felt awful. I shouldn't have come. I hadn't been thinking of Edith's feelings and what she might see. I'd only been thinking of finding Michael.

"It's quite all right. I'm going to keep trying," Edith's voice grew resolute. "I did pick up on something. There's a bar under the Brooklyn Bridge. Maybe that's not the right word for it." Edith thought for a moment. "A club, perhaps I think that's where I was. I heard jazz music and smelled cigarette smoke. I felt like I had been there before, years ago. There was a sense of familiarity. But it was too long ago, and my memory isn't what it used to be." Edith's eyes unfocused once more before snapping back to the present. "Oh, I just don't know!" The poor woman grew angry with herself. Her hand shook as she brought it up to her temple.

"Stop. You can't do this to yourself. You've given Vee plenty of information. I'm sure it will be enough." Karen glared at me from across the table, urging me to speak up and agree.

"Right, you were great. Please, don't exert yourself. Michael wouldn't want you to." I knew that much to be true.

"Come, I think you need to take a rest." Karen helped her grandmother up. Edith didn't fuss. She allowed her daughter to lead her out of the kitchen.

"I'll be back in just a moment," Karen said over her shoulder.

I made my way from the kitchen back out of the living room and onto the front porch. The silence inside the house was too unnerving.

"I'm sorry, I didn't think. I didn't mean to make Edith upset," I said the moment Karen met me outside.

"No, it's okay. I didn't think anything of it either, and it's better that she knows. She might see something else now that she's looking for it."

I nodded, and we were both quiet for a moment.

The wind rustled through the apple trees and caused the grass to sway.

I eventually spoke up. "I have a question. Did you know Michael was working for the agency?" Karen knew all about my work. Michael and I hadn't told her at first. It was against agency rules for me to tell people who I was and where I was from, but the agency couldn't do anything about it when somebody figured it out on their own as Michael had. The fact that he could time jump had come as a complete shock to me. But perhaps it shouldn't have, seeing we shared the same powers. We could both manipulate electricity. Karen insisted she had no desire to see the future, and I respected that.

"Not from him. Sam mentioned it. I figured if Michael wanted me to know, he would've told me."

"Did your husband mention anything about the case Michael was working on?"

"He didn't, but you can bet I'm going to ask him about it now." Karen raised her eyebrows.

"And you'll call me?"

"Are you staying at Michael's?"

"Not right now." I didn't meet Karen's eyes.

"I see."

I don't think Karen did, not exactly, but I wasn't going to elaborate. Mentioning the dead body would only cause Karen to worry more, and I'd grieved Michael's family enough for one day.

"I'm staying at the Fitzgerald. I'll check in with you tonight if I don't talk to you before then." I turned to walk back to the car.

"Hey, Vee?" Karen called out after me.

I turned around halfway to the car, "Yeah?"

"Bring my brother home safe, won't you?"

"I plan on it," I managed to reply before turning back around and walking silently to the car. I waited until I was safely down the road before the first tear fell.

Chapter 7

I wasn't sure how many bars or nightclubs were close to the Brooklyn Bridge in 1964, but I was about to find out. Edith mentioned something about hearing jazz. Perhaps there was a jazz club amongst them. I wasn't sure what to make of the cigarette smoke. It seemed everyone smoked in the sixties, even in restaurants and bars. Traffic was also a nightmare regardless of the decade. By the time the Brooklyn Bridge was in sight, I had spent over five hours in the car for the round trip. Unfortunately, it might be six hours before the bumper-to-bumper traffic moved again. At least the drive gave me plenty of time to think.

I prayed Deacon would come through and give me the case file Michael had been assigned. The agency had only denied my request one time, and that was regarding the case my mother was working when she went missing, but that didn't mean I didn't poke around from time to time trying to uncover the clues. I never got very far. In my mother's case, it wasn't that the agency had abandoned her; they just had nothing to track. They couldn't send any agents after her because they didn't know where she had gone. If I had been older than sixteen, perhaps I would've been strong enough to go after her, but I didn't even know what color her magical signature was. I simply didn't have a thread to chase. Sometimes I dreamt of following a lavender ribbon into the unknown, but I always woke up before reaching the ending and was left wondering about the destination. I shook my head as the dream sequence played out in my head. I had always wondered if that meant that my mother had a lavender signature, but I had never come across it while astral projecting, and she never reached out to me. The only thing I could figure was that she had passed away and no spell could reach her. I swallowed back tears. It had been years since my mother's disappearance made me emotional but adding Michael's trauma to the mix brought a lot of feelings to the surface. I let the thoughts of my mother sink back to the recesses of my memory and decided to focus solely on Michael. I could still save him. Make that, I _would_ save him.

The next question was, which side of the Brooklyn Bridge should I start on? The Brooklyn side or the Manhattan side? In May, 1964, the Verrazzano Bridge wasn't open yet and I didn't want to wait for a ferry from Staten Island to Brooklyn, which meant I would have to cross into Manhattan first. Mind as well start there and let my magic lead me the rest of the way.

I took a moment to sit in the parked car and ground myself. It was hard to do in a place like Manhattan because of the number of people and noise coming at you twenty-four hours a day, seven days a week. Magic could be subtle. You had to quiet your mind to hear it, especially when I was using a spell that relied heavily on my intuition.

I breathed in and breathed out, letting my arms drop into my lap as I pictured Michael's face. The more detail I recalled, the stronger the spell and the better luck I'd have. I imagined Michael driving this very car, the way he would occasionally peer over at me and catch my eye, eyes that were bright blue except for around the iris, where they turned into a smoky gray. Michael had thick dark hair he could style to fit the times, jelled and combed to the side to fit in with the sixties, or tousled in the front when he visited me. The man's looks were versatile. I smiled, thinking about it. My looks hadn't been, not so much anyway. But that had changed. I'd like to think that my appearance hadn't been harsh, but I had to be honest with myself. My once spiky platinum locks and coal-rimmed eyes had morphed. My hair was still short but with soft layers, and I went easy on the eyeliner. When I was feeling philosophical, I liked to think my looks softened the more I let Michael in. I can look back now and realize that I was angry and bitter at the world before I met Michael. There was a reason why I took on the impossible cases. The ones other witches with half a brain would refuse. I had nothing to lose. I hadn't cared what happened to me. I refused to live in fear and let bad guys win, and if that meant that one day, one of them would take me out, then so be it. I was up for the challenge. It was a risk I was willing to take.

But love does something to you. It makes you realize you don't have to push the limit all the time. It's okay to slow down and appreciate life, to let someone in even if it takes a long time and you were never planning on trusting someone in the first place. Not a man anyway.

As I thought about the trust that I had instilled in Michael, I had to believe there was a perfectly good reason why he hadn't told me about working for the agency. In fact, it was the catalyst I needed to get out of my thoughts and get back to tracking him down. You could bet it would be one of the first questions I asked him when I found him.

Universe, I need you
Lead me to Michael
So I can save him

As he's saved me

I took a moment and waited to be directed. Normally, when the spell took root, I'd feel pulled in the correct direction. It often felt as if I had a string coming out of my chest, like a pull-string doll toddling after her owner. But I felt no tug. Nothing told me to move.

I continued to wait and debated saying the spell again, this time with more conviction, when I was suddenly compelled to turn the car back on. I did as I was told. I've been in this business long enough never to second-guess the subtle nudges of the universe.

After looking over my left shoulder, I eased out into traffic and slowly cruised along. "Okay, where are we going?" I asked the unknown.

I continued to focus on the road and where my magic led me, ignoring the pedestrians on their way out to dinner or maybe grabbing a drink after work. Without even thinking, I reached out and turned on my blinker, turning left and getting back on the highway. It looked like wherever I was going, it was on the other side of the bridge in Brooklyn. Again, traffic slowed me down, but I soon found myself taking the first exit after crossing the bridge, parking, and getting out of the car.

I searched my surroundings, trying to figure out where I might be headed—another billiard hall perhaps, or maybe a nightclub. The surrounding area offered plenty of places to grab a drink or catch some music.

After walking a couple of blocks, my feet screeched to a halt. The stop in forward momentum was so unexpected that I stumbled forward to catch my bearings. My eyes had been looking up ahead at a jazz club. I was certain that was my destination. I took several steps back and gazed up at the painted gold sign above the front window. It read Sal's Fine Dining. I leaned forward and took a closer look through the window. The restaurant had a romantic ambiance with white linen-covered tables and soft candlelight. I then looked down at my attire. I wasn't dressed shabbily, but Sal's was the type of place where ladies wore dresses and men donned suit coats and ties. I began to back away to rethink my strategy, but my feet didn't want to budge. It was like trudging through cement. Every step was a chore. "I understand," I mumbled through gritted teeth. "I'm trying to come up with a plan." Where was a ladies department store when you needed one?

"Ah, there we go." I spotted a woman's boutique down the way. It almost appeared to be glowing, like a beacon of hope. Let's just hope they were still open.

Chapter 8

Twenty minutes later, I was wearing a new dress and was ready to play the part. I walked in through the glass-faced front door of Sal's and said hello to the host.

"How many in your party this evening?" he replied.

"I'm meeting someone. Mind if I wait at the bar?" Behind the host's shoulder was an elegantly appointed bar. It was the kind of bar made of hardwood with a brass handrail and dark stain. Clear, blue, and green bottles of top-shelf liquor flanked the cash register. Glassware hung from overhead wracks. Two men worked behind the counter wearing black vests with matching bowties. One man lifted a metal shaker above his shoulder and shook it, sending the ice cubes rattling, while another bent low to talk to a patron.

"Yes, of course, ma'am. Right this way," the host replied. I allowed the gentleman to lead me to the bar and pull back a stool for me to sit on. I thanked him and took my place.

"What are you having tonight, Miss?" The bartender named Sam said to me.

"Gin Martini. Straight up with olives."

"You got it."

"Thanks." I crossed my legs and looked casually around the establishment. I pretended to be waiting for someone to join me. As if Michael would walk through the door, smile, and pull up a seat. Together we would have a drink, maybe an appetizer, before leaving and finding a burger joint or another causal place. It was as good a cover as any and didn't require any additional props to pull off.

"Are you new in town?" Sam asked while straining my drink into a glass.

"No, just don't make it this way all that often. I'm meeting someone for dinner."

"Well, I always recommend the prime rib. You can't go wrong. With the house sauce on top?" Sam kissed his fingertips.

"I'll keep that in mind." I wasn't about to tell the nice man I was a vegetarian. I sipped my martini and tried to get a reading on the place. I wasn't picking up anything supernatural, and the only thing I could smell was the sizzle of steak. That didn't mean much, though; there could be a secret back office or even a basement where Michael might be. The problem was, it was hard to send out feelers into the ethernet without drawing attention to yourself. Most women don't close their eyes and meditate at an upscale bar. I'd end up looking like I was napping or had too much to drink. Neither look was appealing.

"Have you worked here long?" I decided to strike up a conversation with Sam. He stood before me, wiping out the inside of stemware before stacking them on the rack above.

"It's a family business." Sam shrugged his shoulders.

"Ah," I replied, lifting my martini glass, and taking another sip. My intuition was nudging me to continue the conversation. I wasn't sure what else to say, and before I could think of a question, Sam walked away, leaving the bar area, and disappearing off toward the back. I tried not to look disappointed. One thing was for sure, I didn't want to waste my whole evening trying to get Sam's attention. There had to be a quicker way to get the information I needed. If Michael was somewhere in this building, I needed to reach out and find out.

"You mind watching my drink? I'll be back in just a moment," I said to the second bartender as he passed within earshot. He acknowledged that he would, and I slipped off the barstool and headed down a different hallway to the ladies' room. Here, I could lock myself into a stall and reach out to Michael.

Thankfully, the other stalls were empty. Nothing like a flushing toilet to help you lose your focus.

I easily slipped into magic mode.

The moment I closed my eyes and reached out to Michael, I felt his presence. The realization took my breath away. I had to fight the urge to unlock the bathroom stall door and run out of the restroom like a madwoman, turning the place upside down until I uncovered where he was hidden.

I slowed my breathing so I could think clearly.

I wasn't in a safe enough place where I could curl up and astral project. A bathroom stall was no place for such a feat, but I could sense Michael's threads of magic. I closed my eyes and tried to follow them with my mind. They were the palest, thinnest threads, but they were there. I was on the right track, but something still wasn't right. If Michael was here in this restaurant, I should be able to pick up on him, bright and strong. Unless perhaps he was drugged? I had to consider the possibility. I didn't want to think about it, but if Michael was unconscious, his magical signature would be weaker. I needed to act quickly.

As I walked back to my barstool, I came up with a plan. I would finish my drink and then stake out the building, choosing to come back after hours where I could search the establishment without an audience. It was the smartest move.

Sam was back when I took my seat. A black and white photo behind his shoulder caught my eye. "Is that this place?"

"What?" Sam leaned in to hear me better.

I pointed at the picture hanging on the exposed brick wedged between the shelves full of liquor bottles.

"Oh yeah, back in the day when my granddad ran the place, it was a real riot. The basement anyway, we've always served food on the main floor."

"Is the basement still open?"

"No, after prohibition ended, they shut it down. There was no need for it anymore."

"Oh, you mean like a speakeasy." I took a drink of my martini.

"There were gin joints all over the place around here. It's nothing special. It's just storage now."

"Can I see it?"

Sam hesitated. His mouth had been open when I interrupted him with my question. I don't think Sam knew what to make of me.

"I'm a historian," I quickly thought on the fly. "I specialize in the turn of the century. I've always wanted to see a real speakeasy." I know I said I wanted to break in after hours, but I couldn't resist the opportunity Sam presented. If I found something, I could always bewitch the bartender into making him forget me entirely.

"Sure, I guess. Like I said, there's not much left of it, but give me about fifteen minutes, and I can take you down."

"That would be great."

In actuality, it only took Sam about five minutes, and he came back, ready to lead me down the basement stairs. It turned out you accessed the stairwell from the kitchen. No one gave us a second look as we slipped through the alley kitchen and around the corner to the entryway. A series of bare bulbs lined the cinder block wall.

"It was purposely kept plain on this side of things," Sam explained. Even though the club was no longer in use, the stairs were swept clean, and I didn't see any dust or cobwebs. That was a relief. I was a fearless witch except when spiders were involved. Spiders scared me.

There was an empty bookcase on the left-hand side of the wall. The opposite wall held similar shelving lined with heavy stockpots and roasters. Sam pushed on the frame of the empty bookcase, and the door easily swung inward.

My pulse picked up and my heart hammered as each step brought me closer to Michael. Whatever was going on in the basement, Sam was innocent of it. I was sure of it. The young man wouldn't have knowingly led me to a crime scene, and he was way too relaxed talking about the history as he led the way.

"I'm sure you already know this, but prohibition did the exact opposite of what it was supposed to do. Before it, I'm told we only served beer and wine, but during prohibition and ever since, we've been more of a liquor establishment."

I played along like I knew what Sam was talking about. I hoped he didn't ask me for my expertise, seeing he knew more about it than I did.

I was trying to pay attention. Honestly, I was, but on the inside, I was begging my intuition to pick up on a hit. The spell led me here for a reason. Now it was up to me to figure out what that was.

"So, here's the old bar. You can still see the frame of it. We store the extra liquor and bottled beer down here."

I glanced where Sam was pointing but then turned and faced a raised platform, opening my intuition. I could sense Michael, a bit stronger this time, but still not a bull's-eye.

Sam misread my attention. "That's the old stage." he pointed to where I looked. "I wouldn't stand on it now, though. I have no idea how structurally sound it is."

I nodded, or at least I meant to. I'm not sure if I managed to make my head move.

Sam continued. "Then there was a dance floor

here and a bunch of high-top tables. What do you think? Is it how you pictured it?"

It took me a minute to realize Sam had asked me a question. I cleared my throat. "It's a pretty small space."

"You could probably fit about a hundred people down here. Any more than that, and it wouldn't be a secret, you know? Here follow me. There's a hallway back here to a gaming room."

I continued to scan the area with my intuition wide open. The moment I walked through the room's archway, I stopped cold. My head darted around the room. Michael's signature was even stronger here. I tried to keep my expression neutral even as an adrenaline rush coursed through my body.

"Nobody uses the space now?" The room was dark. Sam flicked a switch, but the wayward bulbs did little to illuminate the space. I could make out stacked boxes, broken chairs, and a few tables.

"No, not for years. Why?" Sam looked truly curious.

"It's a feeling I have. I can't explain it. Maybe it's déjà vu."

The ebb and flow of Michael's magic pulsed. It was coming from a back corner. I didn't even think about Sam as I walked forward, my heart in my throat. There was a door. I gripped the handle and twisted it open, terrified of what I might find. The door released with a hard click, and I pulled it open and peered inside.

Sam joined my side with a flashlight. "Here." He clicked it on and handed the light over.

I shined the light in the small, four-by-four room and tried to fight off the disappointment that washed over me. It turned out to be nothing more than an empty wine cellar.

I growled in frustration. Once again, I was too late. I wondered if I'd ever find Michael or if I'd always be two steps behind.

Sam looked at me out of the corner of his eye as if he was rethinking this tour. "What's wrong?"

I cleared my expression. "Nothing. I don't know what I was expecting." I realized I had to quit acting like an anxious tourist. It was clear Michael wasn't here, but he had been. Of that, I was certain. I changed my attitude. "This is great. Definitely a piece of history."

Sam seemed to think for a moment. "Yeah, I guess it is. I never thought of it that way."

"Thank you for showing it to me." We began to backtrack through the main club area and through the bookcase.

"Anytime."

"I might take you up on that," I tried to joke. "For a research article, of course." I attempted to clarify.

"I'm sure that would be all right. I might have to check with my father, but it shouldn't be a problem."

Once back upstairs, I paid for my drink and headed out into the night. I was halfway back to Michael's car when I stopped abruptly and looked over my shoulder. I couldn't shake the feeling that someone was watching me. I wasn't one to turn and run, which is why I stood there for a moment and held my ground. If someone wanted a fight, they would get one. I was in no mood to mess around. I stood there on the sidewalk while tourists and locals passed by. They seemed to keep a wide berth, sensing my unease. After a few minutes of standing and waiting, I shrugged my shoulders and continued on my way to Michael's car. My power was on alert the entire time. When in reality, maybe it shouldn't be. For the first time, it occurred to me that if someone was following me, it might be because of my power. Didn't Mr. Rigatti say that the shifters were rounding up powerful witches? If I were smart, I would cloak my magic and not use spells to lead me around town. I tried not to be frustrated with myself as I slipped behind the wheel and headed out, checking my rearview mirror the entire time.

Chapter 9

An idea took hold as I drove to Midtown. I was going to attempt to astral project again to reach Michael. I thought it would be best to try it from his apartment, where his energy was the strongest. Seeing the cleaning crew had already done their job, I hoped that meant there weren't any death cooties lingering around. That, and the dead shifter's friends wouldn't come around looking for him. I didn't need to up the body count in the building. I parked Michael's car in his usual spot and let myself into the building. I was about to unlock the door and step inside when my intuition went off like an alarm. Somebody else was already inside. I could feel it. I let go of the handle and slowly backtracked. Instinctively, I looked to the right and left to see if anyone else was in the hallway, but it was empty. I stood there quietly, seeing if I could hear anything coming from the other side of the door. But the thing about construction in the early nineteen hundreds, when Michael's apartment was most likely built, was that they were built sturdy, with solid lumber and insulation, which meant that I couldn't hear a thing going on from the other side of the door. I had two options, I could go back to the car and wait the person or persons out, or I could kick down the door with my powers blazing, ready to take down whoever was on the other side. Truth be told, I was feeling option number two. My frustrations over the case had reached an all-time high, and I was ready to get some answers.

I rolled my neck and cracked my knuckles. "Let's do this." I threw my hands down at my side with my fingers extended and called forth my power. Electricity was practically snapping out of my fingertips.

Belatedly, I realized that I might be acting a little unhinged. Any normal human could walk out their door and see me standing in the hallway like a crazed woman, thinking I'd lost my mind, and they'd be right. The quicker I moved, the better.

It would've been awesome if I could actually kick down the door, but instead, I put my hand around the doorknob, planning to unlock it with magic, when the door swung in from the other side, pulling me forward with it.

"OOF!" I stumbled across the threshold

"Were you going to stay out there all evening, or

were you coming inside?" Deacon looked at me like I was ridiculous.

"I almost fried you!" I shot back. I shook my hands out, willing the energy to dissipate.

"I don't know why. I told you I would look into the case and get back to you."

"I thought a case file would magically appear like it usually does," I confessed.

"This time, it's a little different. You owe me." Deacon pointed to the file on Michael's kitchen table.

"What do you mean?"

"The agency isn't sanctioning your involvement." Deacon looked away, not meeting my eyes.

"You stole the file?" I smiled. The motion felt good. Deacon, the most straitlaced program manager I knew, was coming over to the dark side. "Looks like you have a little bit of rebel in you after all."

"I'm only doing this because you have a right to know," Deacon replied defensively. His remark sobered me. "That, and if anyone can find Michael, it's you."

I pulled the case information out of the white sealed envelope and scanned its contents.

"Michael was tracking a missing high priestess?" I continue to read on. I had some knowledge of the coven hierarchy in the area from a previous case. Although, I didn't know this woman personally. The woman had dark hair and deep brown eyes. She looked at the camera with kindness in her eyes. My heart went out to her.

"Celeste was kidnapped by a pack of shifters," Deacon confirmed.

"And you think that's why they took Michael?"

"Maybe he got too close."

I thought for a moment. "It fits with what I already know."

"What do you already know?"

I kept my source confidential, but I went on to tell Deacon about the warlock forcing shifters to kidnap witches. "Either the shifters kidnapped Michael because he was in their way, or they collected him for his power." Regardless, it wasn't good.

"Merrick," Deacon supplied.

"Pardon me?"

"Keep reading. Merrick is the dark warlock responsible. Or at least that's the name he used last time. He changes it up from one decade to the next. I wasn't sure at first, but after we found the frozen shifter den, I can't think of anyone else it would be. There's a photo."

I looked back into the envelop. Sure enough, there was a second photo. This man oozed arrogance. From the smart way he dressed to the cocky glare he shot the camera. He instantly made my skin crawl. "The agency knows about him?"

"And they don't do anything about him. Not anymore. It's a death sentence."

I brushed the tip of my tongue along the roof of my mouth while I thought.

"You don't have to do this," Deacon sought me out with his eyes. "No one would blame you for walking away."

"I would. I would never forgive myself if I didn't at least try."

Deacon sighed. "I knew you were going to say that. I had to at least try."

DEACON LEFT SHORTLY after but not before reminding me that I was on my own. I almost felt sorry for the man. He looked so sad, abandoning me. It wasn't his fault. He couldn't make the agency assign me the case. Just like the agency couldn't force me to leave. There was something strong to be said about having free will. As Deacon left, I thought about what I knew. Shifters were kidnapping witches and warlocks. Those who didn't became Merrick's enemies. The shifters had kidnapped Michael to either get him out of the way or turn him over for his power. I was leaning more towards the power angle, but maybe it was a little bit of both. Regardless, Michael had been in that cellar.

The question was, where was he now, and how could I find him? I had tried scrying and spell work, not to mention Edith's attempt. I was running out of options. There was only so much one witch could do, which is why I was back to trying astral projection. I was counting on my magic being recharged enough from yesterday's time jump to locate him this time.

I had spent enough time in Michael's apartment in the past to feel comfortable in the space. Well, except for yesterday. But I couldn't let one dead body in a closet ruin the memories Michael and I had shared there. I was made of stronger stuff than that.

Before attempting the spell, I placed a quick ward on Michael's front door. I wanted to magically secure the place before going under. In my mind, I hammered magical nails around the doorframe. I then sealed the spell with an electrical field, adding another layer of protection. If someone was still looking for magic, they might sense it coming from the apartment, but they wouldn't be able to reach me.

I crawled into Michael's bed and wrapped myself up in his comforter, breathing in his scent. Being cocooned in this space felt like coming home, only I wished I could bury my face against his chest and not his pillows. I hugged his pillow to my chest while lying on my side and let my mind wander. I picked up the strands of Michael's magic almost instantly. Both of ours filled the space. They twisted and turned, weaving together, creating the thread of life. In my mind, I unraveled my thread from Michael's and wrapped his around my palm. I allowed the energy to pull me through space. Just as before, colors began to swirl in my vision. It was like being dragged through a spring watercolor palette. I willingly went along on the journey. Soon, Michael's apartment was far below me.

"Take me to Michael," I pleaded with the universe. "Show me where he is."

The thread moved faster. Colors blurred as I accelerated, finally tipping forward like on a roller coaster when the cart spills you over the edge and plunges you down the hill. I shot through the darkness. I shut my eyes tightly as the swirls turned to waves. The line went up and down, making my stomach drop each time. After going around in circles for a few moments, I realized that I wasn't getting anywhere. The thread seemed to circle on into eternity. I was spinning off into the unknown with no end in sight. I couldn't understand what was going on. All I knew was I was getting dizzier by the second.

"Michael!" I called out. My voice sounded muffled like I was screaming underwater.

"Detective Cooper!" I tried again. Still, there was nothing. I did the only thing I could think of and pictured my magical thread coming out of my fingertips and weaving with Michael's. It might not lead me to him, but maybe somehow, he would know that I was searching for him.

I followed the thread back. Slower this time. Until I was sinking back into Michael's apartment, into his bed, and back into my body. Spent, I couldn't even open my eyes. Instead, I fell into a deep sleep.

Chapter 10

The next morning, I woke up feeling shaky. My eyes blinked the room into focus. Without a window, it was impossible to tell what time it was. I glanced over at the analog clock in the kitchen, and I could see that it was already after 9 AM. I couldn't believe I'd slept twelve hours. I lay back in the bed and pulled the covers up over my shoulder as I thought through what had happened last night. Disappointment was heavy in my heart, but it had to compete with the dizziness in my head. It took me a minute to realize that I hadn't eaten much yesterday. I was going to have to do something about that quickly, just like I knew that I was going to need some more firepower to locate Michael. I knew I shouldn't reach out to my fellow witchy agents seeing this was an unauthorized case. Lexi would come; I knew she would, even if it was against the rules.

But then I remembered I knew some strong local witches. Irene Hendrick came to mind, along with the two other young women I had rescued from the Catskills. They were a lead worth exploring. Not only that, they were powerful, and I wouldn't have to attempt to astro project again to reach out to them. Not that I could even manage it right now. If I ever had an out-of-body experience again, it would be too soon.

I was still wearing the dress I had purchased the night before.

As this was the start of my third day working the case, I was in dire need of some supplies. I had left in such a hurry that I hadn't bothered with any extra clothes or toiletries. I splashed water on my face and stole a swish of Michael's mouthwash before unlocking the wards and heading out. I kept my head down and Michael's car keys in my hand, heading directly for his vehicle. It was as I was pulling the driver's side door shut after me that I spotted the young blonde-haired woman peek out from around the corner. Our eyes met, and she quickly ducked back. Something about her behavior led me to believe she was the person I'd been sensing. I got out of Michael's car and jogged back across the street, ready to confront her. But when I rounded the corner, I saw that she was gone. I looked down the alley, but there wasn't any place for her to hide unless she was crouched behind a trash can, and even then, she'd have to fold herself in tightly.

"Hello?" I called out anyway. Of course, there wasn't a response. I hadn't expected one. I tried to decide if it was worth running through the alley and tracking her down or if buying clean underwear and getting something to eat was more important. The underwear won out.

There's something oddly comforting about shopping in the sixties. Maybe it was how cheap everything seemed or how friendly the sales associates were, but it never ceased to amaze me how kind people could be. No one's face was buried in a phone, and there was something refreshing about that. People smiled at one another. I also felt comfortable in Michael's neighborhood. I knew the best place to go to get a bagel and who also had the strongest coffee.

I FELT ALMOST human by the time I had eaten and freshened up. With renewed confidence, I headed to Manhattan's Upper West Side. It had been a minute since I had traveled this way. But here, the apartments were much nicer and more expensive. Potted greenery flanked the apartment doors, and men stood at the ready to hold open the door and greet you. I stopped by my favorite newspaperman's stand and said hello before heading into the Hendrix building.

Hey Sid, good to see you." I said after he finished with the customer before me.

"Vee, is that you? It's been a bit."

"It has. How are you?" Sid's gout was known to flare up from time to time.

"Oh, can't complain. I'm getting by."

"And how's the help?"

"I've got a couple of good ones now. Sid motioned with his head down the sidewalk where a redheaded boy was holding up a newspaper, sending customers his way.

"Nice. I'm happy to see that. I was wondering, can I get a copy of The Daily?"

"Sure thing." Sid ducked behind the counter and retrieved a rolled-up newspaper tied with twine. The daily was a supernatural news sheet. You wouldn't find it advertised out front with the regular papers. I handed over a quarter and told Sid to keep the change.

Sid leaned in across the counter. "You stay safe now. Things aren't looking so good around here."

I kept my voice equally low. "I know. What have you heard?"

"It's all in the paper. They say shifter gangs are robbing people now. Not just supernaturals."

"That's risky."

"I know. I'm sure your boyfriend has his hands full at the station."

My mouth was open, but at that moment, I couldn't remember what I was going to say. I wasn't sure if I should tell Sid that Michael was missing or not. It turned out I didn't have to.

"Oh no, what's wrong? I can't have a girl crying at my stand," Sid said playfully to lighten the mood.

I used my knuckle to wipe away a stray tear. "I'm sorry. It's just that Michael's missing. It looks like the shifters took him." I managed to get out.

"Oh sweetheart, that's awful. And you're trying to find him?"

I nodded, unable to speak.

"If anyone can find him, I know you can. I remember how you found that Hendrick girl."

"That's why I am here. I'm hoping to get some help."

"I won't keep you then. But, if I hear anything, I'll let you know."

I swallowed, still regaining my composure. "I'm staying at Michael's. Here, let me jot down the number." Sid turned a notepad my way and removed a pen from behind his ear. I took the pen and scribbled down the digits. "If you hear anything else about what the shifters are up to, anything at all, give me a call."

"Will do. I'll be thinking of you."

"Thanks, Sid," I managed a weak smile and

then turned and walked away. I knew the front doorman at the Hendrick's apartment, having worked there two years ago. But the elevator operator was someone different. Poor Henry must've retired. I sure hoped he was doing all right and that his memory loss had slowed down. He was a rather nice man, and I never did get a chance to thank him for his tip that helped crack open that first case.

"Here goes nothing," I mumbled as I stepped off the elevator, adjusted my shirt, and squared my shoulders. As I walked down the carpeted hallway, I started to think that maybe I should've splurged on a hat and gloves. If anything, Mrs. Hendrick was proper. I wasn't sure how she would react to me showing up on her doorstep and if she would agree to see me at all. Regardless, she wouldn't be happy. I may have saved her daughter's life, but Mrs. Hendrick was the type of person who would want to brush that fact under the rug. It wouldn't be a topic of conversation she would ever want to speak about, let alone have the undercover agent randomly appear two years later. It wouldn't be appropriate conversation. I'm sure that if Mrs. Hendrick thought of me at all, it was as my undercover role as her previous housekeeper. Her husband, on the other hand, probably didn't even remember that much. Mr. Hendrick was a workaholic; he was obsessed with his scientific theories and alchemy. I doubted much had changed in the years since.

Oh well, I was still going to give it a shot. I wasn't sure if Irene still lived with them or if she and Archie were already married. Hopefully, the couple lived somewhere in town, and the Hendricks would agree to put me in touch with them.

I knocked decisively on the door. Moments later, Mrs. Hendrick opened the door. That was the first surprise. I had been expecting a housekeeper. As far as I knew, Mrs. Hendrick didn't answer the door unless it was a last resort.

"My word, it's you." Mrs. Hendrick's eyebrows rose in surprise. I didn't even get a chance to speak before she threw her arms around me and pulled me tightly to her chest. "Frank!" The woman yelled over her shoulder without even letting me go. "Frank! You're never going to guess who's here. It's —" Mrs. Hendrick held me at arm's length and looked down at me. "Well, I don't know your name. I just know that it's not Anna."

"No, it's not," I confessed.

Mrs. Hendrick took me gently by the hand and led me inside the apartment. "Let me put on the coffee. I have so many questions for you."

"You don't have to go through the trouble," I said while surveying the apartment. I looked around for any sign of a housekeeper or Irene, but it looked like Mr. and Mrs. Hendrick were alone. Mr.

Hendrick came out of the living room with a book in hand and greeted us in the kitchen.

"It's Anna," Mr. Hendrick said with a smile.

"Only her name's really not Anna," Mrs. Hendrick looked at her husband knowingly, as if reminding him.

"No, it's not. My name's Vee Harper. I was an agent assigned to your daughter's case."

"I know. We learned all about the Agency of Paranormal Particularities after you left. But no matter how hard we tried, they wouldn't tell us who you were or how to contact you. We both hoped we would get a chance to one day thank you."

I had to admit that the situation was a bit unusual. Normally, once I left a case, I never returned. It was one of the things that I liked so much about the job. I would jump back in time, solve the case, and disappear. I never had to answer any questions or see the same people again. It was a perfect job for someone who hated dealing with emotions and answering questions. But now, I found myself in the exact same situation I had always wanted to avoid, and the funny thing was, it wasn't uncomfortable at all. I was happy to see the Hendricks and even more so when I realized how much the couple had changed. It was apparent by the way they had greeted me and the looks they now shared. Not to mention the tears of gratitude that welled up in Mrs. Hendrick's eyes as she thanked me again and again for saving her daughter's life.

"Does Irene still live here by chance?" I asked

"Oh, no. She has a place with her girlfriends now," Mrs. Hendrick said.

"It's in The Village, which isn't the best part of town." Mr. Hendrick lifted his hand and tilted it from side to side, gesturing that it was so-so. "But we know our girl can handle herself."

"Her and Archie?" I started to ask.

"They broke up all on their own." Mrs. Hendrick shook her head as if she couldn't believe it either.

"I found that most odd." Mr. Hendrick adjusted his tie with his free hand. "She said she loved the boy, but once we gave our blessing, she decided she just wasn't that much into him." Mr. Hendrick shrugged.

"Oh, I was hoping I could speak with her. Could I possibly get her phone number or address from you? If not, can you give her my number and tell her to give me a call?"

"You're in town now?" Mrs. Hendrick looked excited.

"My boyfriend lives nearby."

"Well, that's just wonderful. We'll have to have you over for dinner sometime."

Mr. Hendrick looked unsure. His wife caught his

expression, and hers turned sheepish. "Or maybe we'll go out."

"We never bothered to rehire a housekeeper," Mr. Hendrick added.

"And what my husband is trying not to say is that I am a horrible cook." The two lovingly looked at one another.

"Going out to dinner would be great." I didn't want to tell the Hendricks that Michael was missing. They seemed so excited and happy to see me. I didn't want to dampen their joy. Besides, it just gave me added motivation to find Michael. Like I needed anymore, but that was beside the point.

"Let me get her information for you," Mrs. Hendrick said.

Chapter 11

I left the Hendrick's shortly after that with Irene's contact information tucked in my pocket. Mrs. Hendrick promised to call soon with a dinner invitation, and I told her I was looking forward to it.

I drove a direct route to Irene's apartment and hoped that she would be home. Mrs. Hendrick had offered to call her daughter, but I told her it wasn't necessary. However, I bet any amount of money that she had done just that the moment she shut the door after me.

Greenwich Village was not a bad part of town, not like East Harlem was. You wouldn't find graffiti, litter, or cars perched on cinder blocks. It might not be as nice as the Upper West Side, but then again, what place was other than the Upper East Side? If you asked me, Greenwich Village in 1964 *was* the sixties. Here you had music, and politics, and art—the good stuff.

The second I knocked on Irene's door, and she opened it up, I knew my assumption was right. "I can't believe it's you," she said, copying her mother and embracing me. "Melanie, Patty, she's here!" Irene took me by the hand and led me into the living room. The apartment was small but cozy. The walls were painted a buttery yellow. Irene had a vase full of daisies on the coffee table; sunlight from the living room window filtered in on them. The blue velvet couch had white fluffy throw pillows, and a pale blue quilt stylishly draped over the side. The air smelled of fresh-baked chocolate chip cookies, reminding me not to skip lunch. I wasn't sure which one of these ladies was a kitchen witch, but one of them had to be with how warm and inviting the space was.

The women popped their heads out of their rooms. They wore matching broad grins. I recognized them instantly as the two witches I had rescued along with Irene that fateful night.

"Told you she would come back," Melanie replied smugly. Her dark curls bounced above her shoulders as she turned to look at each one of her friends.

"I know. How could we have ever doubted you?" Irene's voice dripped with heavy sarcasm.

"How much do I owe you?" Patty sighed, looking at Melanie.

"Nah, don't worry about it. It was all in good fun." Melanie strolled out into the room but kept her distance, unlike Irene, who still held my hand.

I stood in awe at this trio of women. All three of them had been through so much, and yet here they were, vibrant, smiling, and bantering with one another. Despite the past, they appeared to be thriving.

I hadn't realized how good this visit would be for my soul. Maybe the agency should rethink the whole disappearing act, never-to-be-heard-from-again routine. It wasn't like the families we helped didn't know magic existed. Would telling them about time travel be that much harder for them to grasp? It made me want to reach out to all my previous cases. A fact that shocked me, but maybe it shouldn't have. I had grown a lot over the past two years. The self-realization made me proud.

"Sorry, don't mind us," Irene apologized, finally letting go and stepping to the side. "I couldn't believe it when Mama said you stopped by. We were getting ready to head out shopping, but we made sure to stay put."

"We didn't want to miss you," Patty said, still smiling.

"I honestly can't tell you how good it is to see you guys and how great you look," I confessed.

The three ladies blushed. They had blossomed into young women since the last time I saw them.

"I don't think we can thank you enough for what you did," Irene started to say.

"Although, I think we could have taken them," Melanie shrugged.

"Uh, do you remember those shifters? It was a full moon!" Patty's eyes grew wide.

"Patty's right. We could've taken down Mary, but not the shifters. We would've been toast if it wasn't for you and your friends," Irene added.

I thought back to the girls' rescue and remembered how my friends Lexi, Nuala, and Michael all played a part.

"Mama said your name is Vee?" Irene asked.

"Vee Harper," I clarified.

"And you work for that secret agency," Patty said with more enthusiasm than I'd ever heard from anyone referencing The Agency.

"You should have her head up your recruitment department." Melanie looked at her friend and shook her head. "She's determined to be one of you one of these days."

"Do you think I have what it takes?" Patty's eyes were full of hope. With those doe eyes, I would've told her yes even if I didn't think she stood a chance. But the truth was, any one of these women could work for the agency. I told them as much. Patty clapped her hands with excitement. "Here, let me go get my resume," she ducked back into her room.

"She's been obsessed with solving cases ever since she learned about the agency," Irene supplied.

"Let's hope Agatha Christie doesn't stop writing anytime soon," Melanie quipped.

"Speaking of mysteries," I segued into the reason for my visit. "I'm trying to solve one. What do you guys know about a kidnapped high priestess?"

Melanie looked at Irene. "I told you she wasn't here for a social visit." Melanie didn't look angry, only smug.

Irene ignored her friend. "We know all about Celeste. That's why we're going shopping together. It's not safe to be solo these days."

"Especially for someone like you. It's the powerful ones they're after," Melanie said to me.

"Does this mean you need our help?" Excitement gleamed in Patty's eyes as she rejoined us, a typed-up resume in her hand. She must have overheard the conversation from her room.

"That's kind of what I was hoping for," I admitted as I took the paper from her hand.

I went on to tell the trio about Michael and what I knew about the shifters and Merrick.

"We need to go to Sera," Irene said to Patty and Melanie when I finished.

"Who's Sera?" I asked.

Melanie groaned. "Not Sera. She's always so bossy. I hate being told what to do."

"That's because you have a problem with authority," Patty remarked knowingly.

Melanie glared at her friend. "What's wrong with that? Rules are meant to be broken," she grumbled.

I could see how Melanie gave her foster parents a run for their money, and Michael too. She had run away from home more than once. Michael said he had tried to introduce her to a local coven to help set her on the right path, but it sounded like that hadn't worked out either.

"Sera is a high priestess here in The Village. She's wicked smart, but she expects hard work if you hope to hone your craft." Irene said the last part to Melanie, who rolled her eyes in return. "She's the one that warned us to be careful."

"I'm sure Sera will know how to track Michael," Patty said cheerfully.

"I say let's go to Sera then." If there was one thing I'd learned over the last few days, it was that I couldn't do this alone. I avoided looking at Melanie when I spoke. It looked like someone still had a bit of growing up to do.

AN OLDER WOMAN with flowing silver hair and chunky turquoise jewelry opened the door. She wore a red floral dress hidden under a black apron splattered with paint like a palette. The woman's eyes were strikingly blue as she assessed me. "Girls, what can I do for you?" She never took her eyes off me.

"This is my friend, Vee. Remember I told you about the witch who saved us? Vee, this is Sera," Irene completed the introductions.

"Ah, the time traveler. Your aura now makes more sense," Sera seemingly relaxed, opened the door the rest of the way, and welcomed us inside.

Sera's studio apartment was a feast for the eyes. Large, black-framed industrial windows let in an abundance of light, bathing her artwork in an earthy glow. My eyes were drawn to the Impressionist-styled paintings. Some of which were larger than me in both height and width. The paintings appeared three-dimensional with the painting technique Sera employed. It looked like she used a putty knife instead of a paintbrush. Sera's use of color captivated me. The face-sized dahlias were especially breathtaking. The base of one of the blooms was a Persian blue that gradated to periwinkle before fading to lilac. Pops of green and yellow radiated from the deep violet center. The painting made me stop and wonder if anyone else had ever captured the flower's beauty more perfectly. I was truly captivated. And that was only the first painting that caught my attention. My eyes scanned the space. Sera had artwork displayed throughout her home. Oversized canvases hung against the exposed brick walls, and framed prints sat on the coffee table. Sera had even painted the bedroom partition, and she had more finished canvases stacked in the corner. The entire apartment looked like studio space except for the bedroom.

"Are you an artist?" Sera asked me while Melanie, Irene, and Patty settled themselves on the white canvas sofa and loveseat. The white furniture made the walls stand out even more.

"Not even remotely. Your work is stunning." I couldn't tear my eyes from the walls.

"Thank you. It helps to have an outlet for when I can't sleep at night, and my magic is as restless as my mind. When I turn to the canvas, it soothes me."

I nodded wordlessly.

"You should try it sometime. You might like it."

I wasn't sure about that. I had plenty of restless nights. But I struggled for a way to see how painting could apply to me. I had my job, and I had Michael. That was enough.

Sera looked at me with raised eyebrows.

"We'll see." Maybe I shouldn't be so quick to dismiss Sera. Perhaps I needed something more, something to calm me and bring me joy.

I shrugged.

Or maybe not. Because catching bad guys sure

did bring a smile to my face. As did making the world a better place.

"Think about it," Sera said softly.

"I will, promise."

"So, how can I help you?" Sera and I continued to have a side conversation away from the other girls.

"My boyfriend's been kidnapped by a pack of shifters. At least, that's what I think happened. He was working a case for my agency about a missing high priestess, Celeste."

"Ah, poor Celeste. I've been looking for her every night, but she has yet to come to me." Something about the way Sara worded her statement made me think she meant she was looking for Celeste through metaphysical means.

"It's the same with Michael. I've tried astral projection and scrying, but I can't pinpoint his location. I stopped by Irene's, hoping she would lend me some of her power. She suggested we come to you."

"What happened when you projected to him?"

"I could trace his magic, but I ended up spinning off into nowhere. I can't explain it any better than to say that I felt like I was stuck."

"That's what happened when I projected to Celeste. She's a sweet witch. I've known her for years and can pick up her magical trace as clear as my own, but even I couldn't follow her into the unknown."

"Perhaps together?" I motioned to the other witches sitting on the couch. Witchcraft 101, witches were always stronger together.

"Perhaps," Sera agreed. "Tell me about the night he went missing."

I went on to retell how Michael woke me from my sleep and what had happened since. I even told Sera about the frozen shifter den and the dark warlock, Merrick.

"Over the years, I've heard rumors about him. He runs hot and cold, striking a community and then disappearing for decades. I'd always assumed he was an urban legend until recently."

I then thought of something. "Do you know any spells that leave blue smoke behind?"

"Blue smoke? Freezing spells do. Which would make sense in the gaming den, but not in the alleyway."

"Any transportation spell? Michael can time jump like I can, but I doubt he would've pulled the shifters with him, and it wouldn't have resulted in the smoke." I was talking the case out for Sera as much as for myself.

"Hmm, we could do an energy recreation spell. That might let us slow things down and see what happened in the alley."

"I hadn't thought of that." We probably would need a few more extra witches to pull that off. Whenever something happened that expelled a bunch of energy, it left an imprint on the environment. Witches could tap into that energy and play-back the scene. I wondered if that's what I had seen when Michael projected for help. It would make sense. The ether thrived on energy. It could have easily played back what was happening.

"Except, I doubt the energy's still there." Sera seemed to be talking to herself as much as to me. "It's outside, and it's been two days. The energy would have dissipated by now. It would be different if it happened inside an enclosed area, like an apartment," Sera remarked.

Her comment had me thinking about the dead shifter in Michael's closet. I had left that part out in my retelling. We could use the spell to re-create the murder in the apartment, but I didn't say anything to Sera. I wasn't sure how much I wanted her to know, and I wanted a chance to talk with Michael first.

"Well, whatever spell we decide to go with, we'll need every witch we can muster. Let me activate the phone tree." Sera patted me on my hand and then turned to walk away. I watched as she slipped behind the partitioned section of the room and moments later heard her make that phone call.

<hr>

Chapter 12

<hr>

I quickly recognized the benefits of having a larger living space as witch after witch filed through Sera's front door. As someone who had always been a solo practitioner, the coven mentality was foreign to me. These men and women had no idea who I was, and yet they had dropped everything to come and help a total stranger. I kept smiling and nodding as I was introduced to each person, not remembering half of their names. It turned out Patty was the kitchen witch. The moment Sera said she was calling a full coven meeting, Patty hopped off the couch and started preparing snacks. Sera didn't bat an eye as Patty rummaged through her kitchen cupboards, pulling out platters and Tupperware bowls. Within fifteen minutes, Patty had prepared a veggie tray, a fruit tray, and chips with accompanying dips before turning her attention to beverages. It seemed high priestess always had to have the kitchen stocked for impromptu gatherings. I was a little iffy on my coven hierarchy, but usually, to be a coven leader, you had to be a third-degree practicing witch, otherwise known as a high priestess. I didn't really care what Sera's title was, only that her intentions were good, and her power was strong. I was putting a lot on the line trusting these people. I hoped it didn't backfire.

I was grateful when Sera recapped why she had called the meeting and saved me from explaining the situation once more. Sera's summary was even more succinct, letting the members know that we were trying to find Michael and Celeste as well. Sera looked at me, daring me to object, but I was silent. I had no problem searching for Celeste <u>after</u> I found Michael.

"Eat up," Sera finished off by saying. "You're all going to need your strength if we're going to get this spell to work. You too," Sera said to me in a softer voice.

I smiled politely in return. I didn't have much appetite, and I didn't feel like sitting around and wasting time while everyone ate, but Sera had a point. I wasn't about to give up years of being a vegetarian and dive into a ham sandwich, but I did grab a handful of carrots and nibbled on some chips.

It was then, as I was washing it all down with a

glass of lemonade that the young girl who had been following me walked through the door. Our eyes locked like the day before, and the girl immediately turned tail and slipped out the front door.

"Abigail!" Sera shouted after the young girl. Sera glanced around the room to see if she could figure out what had spooked Abigail before running after her.

I wasted no time dashing after them both.

Abigail had the door to the stairwell open and was about to run down the stairs when Sera caught up with her. I was two seconds behind.

"Wait! I need to talk to you," I shouted.

Sera looked back at me. She hadn't realized I'd followed them out. I continued, "You've been following me, and I want to know why." My voice came out harsher than expected. Tears piled up in the corner of the girl's eyes and spilled down her cheeks.

I quickly backtracked at Sera's reproving look. "Sorry, I didn't mean it like that. But you have been following me for the last two days. I want to know what's going on."

"Abigail, what's wrong?" Sera spoke over me. Her demeanor was much softer.

"They took mama," she managed to say, her voice trembling.

Sara gasped. "Not Rachel."

Abigail nodded. The tears continued to fall freely down her face.

"The shifters kidnapped your mother?" I wanted to make sure I understood Abigail.

She wiped her cheeks with the sleeve of her shirt. "I was waiting for her in the car when she went in to talk to Detective Cooper. She never came back out. I don't know what's happened to her or where she is." Abigail turned to me. "You're the only person I've seen go in and out of the apartment since."

"No one else is in the apartment. I have no idea what happened," my response was directed more towards Sera, who was looking at me for the answers. There was the whole dead shifter to still account for. Could Abigail's mom have killed him and then ran, leaving her daughter behind? It was one possible scenario. I wasn't going to suggest that theory in front of Abigail.

Instead, I did my best to soften my voice like Sera had and looked down at Abigail. The young girl couldn't be much older than fifteen. Ironically, she was about the same age I was when my mother had vanished. "Detective Cooper is missing too. That's why I am here. I came to find him."

"Then you have to find mama. They must be together. Don't you think?" The words rushed out of Abigail's mouth.

"It's a possibility." I carefully measured my

response. If Rebecca didn't kill the shifter and run away, she could have also been kidnapped. I reminded myself not to assume anything.

"Then I'm coming with you. Wherever you're going, I'm following." Abigail pointed her finger at her chest and stood defiantly.

I looked over at Sera for a little bit of help here. I was in over my head as it was. There was no way I could be responsible for a young witch's life too.

"Abigail, it's too dangerous. Vee is a professional, but even she can't keep you safe."

"Sera's right. I'd never forgive myself if something bad happened to you."

"I don't need your protection. I can look after myself. What do you think I've been doing the past two days? I've been on my own, and I've been just fine."

"You should've come to me. You don't have to be brave alone. That's what we're here for." Sera reached over and gave Abigail a hug. The young girl welcomed the embrace and rested her head on Sera's chest.

After they stepped apart, Abigail looked up at me expectantly.

"I promise I'll do whatever I can to find your mother. You have my word as a witch, and that's pretty big," I vowed.

Abigail looked unsure, but this time she didn't voice her opinion.

"Why don't you go inside and get something to eat. We'll start the circle soon," Sera dismissed Abigail and then turned to me. "What aren't you telling me?" she asked the moment we were alone.

I didn't try to deny it or beat around the bush. "I found a dead shifter in Michael's closet."

Sera didn't miss a beat. "You think Rebecca might have something to do with it?"

I shrugged my shoulders. "I didn't even know Rebecca existed until five minutes ago. But, maybe they tried to kidnap her inside Michael's apartment, and she killed the shifter and ran. I'm not sure. I can tell you she wasn't in the alleyway when Michael vanished. And no one was at his apartment when I got there shortly after."

Sera took a deep inhale through her nose while she thought. "I don't think Rebecca would've abandoned her daughter, even if she killed someone."

"Not even if she thought she was protecting her?"

Sera's expression looked unsure.

"The best thing we can do now is find Michael, and hopefully, he'll lead us to the others."

Sera nodded, and we went back inside to rejoin the group.

Chapter 13

Every magical community has its own way of doing things, and seeing I was a guest, I left it to Sera to get things going. The coven members had already pushed the couch, loveseat, and coffee table against the walls, leaving the wide plank scarred wood floors bare. Like a coordinated dance, each witch took their place and formed an outside circle. Irene and Patty held their hands open for me to join them. Sera looked at me and nodded approvingly, and I did just that.

Sera walked around the outside of the circle, blessing and securing the space. Then she placed a gold-framed rectangular mirror on the floor in front of me. When she was done, she looked over at me expectantly.

Unfortunately, I had no idea what she wanted me to do.

"Perform the spell," she said gently. "We will lend you our powers. Just don't let go."

"Oh, okay." I tried not to look at the twenty pairs of eyes staring at me in anticipation. Well, make that eighteen pairs of eyes. Two of the witches already had their eyes closed in concentration. My mouth suddenly felt very dry. There was nothing like performing for an audience. Did I mention that I was completely outside of my comfort zone?

But I had to block everything out and focus solely on finding Michael. He was all that mattered. I wished I had his badge with me or something else I could use to focus on. Instead, I could only hope the coven's power would be strong enough.

Irene squeezed my hand, which was all the encouragement I needed to proceed. I repeated the spell I had used before when I was scrying for Michael in his bathroom.

Power I need, come to me.

With harm to none, so mote it be

As I continued on with the spell, I felt the group's power pulse into me. One after another, they sent their strength to me.

Show me Michael here and now

So I may save him

Free from sorrow

Safe at last

Undo the past

And set him free

As I will it, so mote it be.

Jazz music floated in the background. It was muffled, not because of the spell, but because of where Michael was. I was close to seeing him, but he still was out of focus. I tried again.

Sharpen the image, make it more clear

Show me Michael Cooper, the detective I hold dear.

As the power hummed and the energy built within me, the picture became crystal clear. I was right. Michael was in the basement of Sal's, only he wasn't in 1964. He was in a different year.

He was stuck sometime during prohibition. He had to be.

I dropped to my knees. My fingertips reached out to the mirror as if I could psychically link with Michael and discover what year he was trapped in. But the moment I broke contact with the circle, ungrounded power erupted and blew everyone back until we were all left on our backsides.

A variety of shrieks and creative curses punctuated the air. "Sorry," I said breathlessly. "I know where he's at. I don't know the exact year. But that's okay. I'm going to find him." The words rush out of my mouth in a single breath. I knew I might not be making that much sense, but right then, I didn't have time to explain. I would fill Sera in once Michael was back home safe and sound. I stood up and surveyed the group. They were still regaining their balance and strength. I didn't realize until then how much of their energy the spell had drained. On the other hand, I felt like a nuclear reactor ready to power a city. I was powerful and invincible with the coven's energy mingling with my own. If there ever was a time to jump back and kick butt, this was it.

"Where is he?" Sera was the first to ask.

"He's at Sal's. It was a speakeasy back in prohibition. I tracked him there yesterday, but I couldn't find him. His energy was there. I assumed he had already been moved. It never occurred to me that he was still there, but in a different year."

"But what year?" Sera asked.

I shook my head. "I'm not sure. I'll hop from year to year until I find him." I was running on pure adrenaline.

"You can't do that. Prohibition lasted over a decade. Even you can't time jump that many times." Melanie looked irked.

I glared at the young witch even though she was right.

"Plus, all the days, it's not just the years," Patty chimed in.

A middle-aged man, I think his name was Paul spoke up. He wore a button-up, short-sleeved, plaid shirt, khakis, and black-framed glasses. He began ticking off numbers on his fingers. "That's thirteen years times 365 days a year to equal 4,745 days."

"Too many days," Sera said, stating the obvious. "We need the exact date."

"How?" I didn't know a single spell that could do that. Michael found me one time. After I pressed him on it, I found out Lexi had given him my contact information. I thought she'd already time jumped ahead of me, but nope. My best friend liked to remind me from time to time she was to thank for our lasting relationship.

"There has to be something." Sera tapped her chin thoughtfully. While everyone sat in silence, literally no one else had bothered to get up off the floor, I was ready to jump back to January 1, 1920. The start of prohibition was as good a time as any. I had opened my mouth, prepared to make my excuses, when Paul spoke up once more.

"What is it, Lester?" Sera asked. I closed my eyes. I was way off on his name.

"What about blood magic? There's that potion, something about tracing your ancestors. Does anyone remember going over this?" Lester looked at his fellow coven members.

"Oh, wait!" Patty stood up with excitement in her voice. "It was one of Merlin's spells, wasn't it? It had all those random ingredients. Like duckweed and frogspawn."

"Precisely. The ingredients aren't hard to come by. They're just not normally on hand," Lester confirmed.

Sera nodded her head. Her fingertips were still resting on her chin.

"Who has a copy of the spell?" Melanie asked skeptically.

"Don't you remember? The New York Public Library has one in their special section." Patty used air quotes around the word special and section.

"This could work," Sera said while staring off into space.

"This is a spell?" I cleared my throat and spoke up. I had never heard of one like it, but I didn't make it a habit to study spell theory and magical history. Perhaps I should.

"It's a potion," Lester clarified.

That explained things even further. I avoided potions at all costs. It was like oil and water. I was better at unlocking doors and scrambling people's memories. A witch played to her strengths, and I knew mine.

"So, wait. How would this work exactly? We needed a drop of Vee's blood?" Patty spoke up once more.

"No, that won't work. It's supposed to be a blood relative. You're not related to this guy, are you?" A witch, who I was pretty sure her name was Veronica, spoke up.

"No, we're not related." That would be awkward. I didn't know my family tree that well. All I knew about my father was that he was a warlock, and a horrible man, who left my mom high and dry after he found out about me. But regardless, I never suspected Michael and I were related.

"How's the spell going to work then?" Melanie looked at all of us like we were a bit daft.

"I'll call his sister. She lives about two hours away. I'm sure she'd be willing to drive up for this. Hands down." No questions asked even.

"That's how," Sera said to Melanie in a stern voice. Melanie snapped her mouth shut. The poor girl really did have a lot to learn, and her attitude wasn't doing her any favors in this life. I learned a long time ago that witches with bad attitudes usually felt wronged by the world. It was no secret that the world had been unkind to Melanie. I wondered what it would take to make her see that it wasn't all bad. I'd have to solve that problem on a different day.

"Here's the plan. Lester, you and Veronica head to the library and copy the spell. Vee will call Michael's sister and see how quickly she can get here. Then together, we'll round up the ingredients and perform the spell at nightfall."

"On the full moon," Irene chimed in.

"Yes, on the full moon. Luna will only help illuminate this mystery tonight," Sera looked out the window as if she could already see the satellite's brightness.

Sera led me to the partitioned area of her apartment. I was right in that it was her bedroom. A banana yellow rotary phone stood out on the empty whiskey barrel she used as a nightstand.

I only hoped Karen's kids were at school once again and the house was quiet enough for her to hear the phone and answer it.

I didn't have to wait long for my answer.

Karen picked up the phone after one ring. "Hey --" I started to say.

"Vee? My goodness, where have you been? I've been trying to call you for two days. You're not staying at the Fitzgerald, are you." I'd completely forgotten to update Karen. She didn't even let me get a word in. "Have you found him?"

"Yes and no. I know where he is, but I don't know when. I need your help."

"I'm on my way," Karen said the second I finished explaining the plan. I handed the phone off to Sera for her to give Karen directions to her apartment.

I wasn't sure what to do with my time after that. I was restless. I wanted to pick a date, jump, and see what I found. Maybe I would get lucky. At this point, I think the universe owed me a favor. But I knew that if Agatha were with me, she would encourage patience, just like Sera had. I tried to hang on to that rationalization as the minutes ticked by.

I had already done the math in my head. It would take Karen at least two hours to reach us. I bet it would take Lester and Veronica about the same time with traffic to and from the library, plus the time it took Lester and Veronica to copy the potion. I had no idea if the duo had to copy by hand or if the library had a copy machine. I knew they were available in the early sixties. Michael had shared what a big deal it was when they got one last year at his precinct. But they still weren't common in the workforce. Basically, what it all boiled down to was I had time on my hands, and I wasn't sure what to do with it. I was thinking about all of this while staring at Sera's artwork once more. I suppose I could get lost in her paintings for a couple of hours. That wouldn't be so bad.

Soon, everyone had left except for Sera and me. Even Irene, Melanie, and Patty were assigned a job. Patty, having remembered quite a few of the potion's ingredients, volunteered the group to go and round up the ones they could find. I assumed they'd be headed down to Chuck's hardware store in Radio Alley. Chuck's was really a front for a metaphysical shop and an impressive one to boot. Normally, I'd be up for a visit, but even witchy wares couldn't hold my interest.

"You should get some rest," Sera said, handing me a porcelain teacup.

"Rest. Are you kidding me?" I took the cup from her anyhow and leaned forward, smelling the lemony scent. "Chamomile?" I guessed.

"For starters. You look anxious, so I mixed a calming tonic. Its effects won't linger, and it won't knock you out, but it will help you relax for a little bit. I think you need it," Sera added when I started to protest.

This was why Sera was a coven leader. Here she was, trying to take care of me, and I wasn't her responsibility.

"Thank you." I closed my eyes and took a sip, letting the warm liquid slide down my throat. I wasn't instantaneously relaxed, but maybe the ice ball stuck in my chest would start to melt.

"This is your job?" Sera said, motioning to me as I exhaled a shaky breath.

"It is, and I know you don't believe me, but I love it. There is no better thrill than bringing justice to this world. I can't explain it. It's what I live for." I didn't hide the passion from my voice.

"Except when a loved one's life is on the line."

I cocked my head. "Except for that."

Chapter 14

I didn't think it was possible, but I did manage to take a nap on Sera's bed. I woke to the gentle murmur of voices on the other side of the partition. It took me a minute to remember where I was, but the moment I regained full consciousness, the dredges of sleep cleared, and I felt fully awake.

"Karen," I said with a smile as I saw Michael's sister.

She met me halfway across the living room and wrapped me in a hug.

"I knew you would find him," she said with confidence. I looked over her shoulder. "I'm surprised you didn't bring Edith."

"Someone has to be home when the kids get off the bus. Sam's already in the city here."

"He is? I haven't seen him." I thought maybe I would have run into him at Michael's. Then again, why would he stop by if he knew his brother-in-law was missing and thought I was staying at the Fitzgerald?

Karen kept her voice low. "Turned out, Michael confided in Sam quite a bit. He came up to lend Michael a hand, and he's been looking for him ever since." I was about to suggest that we should have teamed up. Karen must have read my mind. "I did try to get in touch with you," she reminded me.

I closed my eyes and shook my head. "It's okay. We know where Michael's at right now. We only have to find the right date."

Behind us in the kitchen, five witches stared over a simmering stockpot on Sera's stovetop. There was no cauldron or open flame. It was more of a steel stockpot on a two-burner stove. Lester read off the ingredients and double-checked the measurements as Patty continuously stirred the liquid. I decided I was better off staying right where I was. It looked like there were already too many witches in the kitchen. I would only get in the way.

"Good, you're up." Sera joined us. "I checked the ephemeris and the moon peaks early tonight at 7:52. I've asked everyone to be here by seven."

"Okay, good. What time is it now?" I really had no clue.

Karen looked down at her watch. "It's just before six."

Okay, so that gave me a little over an hour to get

everything together for when I time jumped. I hadn't left anything at Michael's that I might need, but I did have to figure out what to wear. I expressed as much to Karen and Sera, hoping they knew of a local thrift store or maybe Sera had something that would work in her closet. I was guessing her age to be somewhere in her mid-sixties, which meant she would've been in her twenties during the twenties.

"Veronica has you covered. She works as a costume designer on Broadway. She said she'll bring something back with her," Sera replied.

"Oh," I blinked a few times, unsure what else to say.

"See, there are benefits to being in a coven." Sera winked and walked away.

For the record, I never said there weren't benefits to being in a coven. It was more like I wasn't used to working with one, and how did Sera know that?

In no time, the coven had reassembled in Sera's living room. Only this time, the atmosphere was quite a bit more serious. There wasn't a single cup of punch or serving platter set out for members to sip from or munch off. The mood was somber; the members were serious. My nerves ratcheted up a notch. So much was riding on this spell. The outcome could very well determine Michael's fate. I was feeling the pressure.

This time when the coven formed the circle, it

was smaller, tighter. Sera had her makeshift bedside table brought to the center of the floor. Someone had placed a white pillar candle, silver chalice, a palm-sized athame, and paper with the copied spell on it. The oversized windows of the loft were open, letting in the evening breeze. The windows were so tall and wide, and the ceiling so high, it almost felt like being outside.

Sera stood in the center of the circle and motioned for Karen and me to step forward while she worked to magically enclose the space. I peered over the chalice's edge at the darkened liquid inside. It was so thick and dark that I couldn't see the bottom of the cup.

Each witch held a white taper candle. A cardboard disc would keep the wax from dripping on their hands. After sealing the circle, Sera lit a larger white candle with the match from her pocket, striking it on the metal rim of the barrel, sparking the flames to life. In a moment, she lit her candle and then walked it over to Irene to light hers. One by one, the witches turned to each other and passed the flame around, creating a ring of fire.

The ceremonial glow was soothing. Once everything was in place, Sera began to read the incantation.

More than once, Sera paused and held up her hand right hand out, palm up. When she did, the witches replied, "So mote it be."

Karen and I exchanged a look. She had no idea what was going on either. At least that made two of us. After a few minutes, Sera put the paper down and picked up her athame. The ceremonial knife had a double blade and a black handle. Karen readily held her hand out. Sera gently poked her finger and then turned Karen's palm over, squeezing two drops of blood into the chalice. The potion began to hiss. A soft mist stirred in the center of the chalice and began to rise into the air.

I instinctively bent forward to try to peer into the fog and see what secrets it would reveal. But just as quickly as it began to form, the mist faded away.

Sera pursed her lips. I could tell right away that that wasn't how the potion was supposed to work.

Karen held her hand out once more. "You need more blood?"

Sera was thoughtful. "Perhaps, but I don't think it's yours."

"He is my brother. I promise you." Karen faltered. She seemed to think. "The same mother, at the least."

"Calm, child. I don't doubt that Michael is your brother. But I think there's a way we can make the spell stronger." Sera caught my eye.

"Me?" I asked Sera and then looked at Karen to see what she thought of the idea. She shrugged.

"You love him, don't you?" Sera asked.

"Absolutely." Michael and I weren't big on making public displays of affection, but he never had to doubt my feelings. If Karen ever doubted how much I cared for her brother before, it was completely erased now. I held out my palm. "Take what you need."

"Just a little," Sera replied. Just as before, she used the athame to poke the tip of my finger, only this time she squeezed the blood onto the blade and then used it to stir the potion.

The seconds ticked by, and it seemed like the spell was a bust. My heart began to beat funny in my chest as I realized that Michael might be lost to me forever. I was going to suggest we try something else. What that might be, I had no idea, but then the chalice began to froth and bubble.

The mist was back in full force. It swirled out of the cup like a thick fog. It rose in the air above us. It gathered over our heads, forming a cloud in the middle of Sera's living room. Instinctively, the three of us backed up to better see what was happening, but I was careful not to break the circle. I had learned my lesson the last time.

Suddenly, there was a crack of lightning, followed by the low rumble of thunder. The electricity in my body responded in kind. It burned hot. I could taste the static in my mouth.

A second bolt of lightning sizzled in the air.

It was then, in that second burst, that a series of

numbers appeared: 7171927. In a flash, the digits disappeared.

I replayed the numbers in my mind and realized they stood for a date—July 17, 1927. I knew exactly when and where Michael was. Now it was time to jump.

Chapter 15

"You sure this dress is right?" I looked down at the V-neck dress I was wearing. The under shell was a dusty pink color. A mesh layer with heavy black beading and fringe lay over it. The entire dress came just below my knees. A pair of black satin heels completed the look. They reminded me of high-heeled tap shoes.

"You want the headband too?" Veronica asked me, holding up the satin headpiece.

"I think you should wear it," Karen said. "It completes the look."

I still had my doubts, but the quicker I got into costume, the quicker I could save Michael.

I allowed Veronica to fuss over my hair, and I was ready to go two minutes later.

"Here, it's all I have, but you might need it." Karen handed me a handful of cash.

I took the bills and looked down at either side of the dress for a pocket. Coming up empty, I tucked the bills into the front of my dress. "Thank you. I'll pay you back."

"Save my brother, and you can keep it." Karen tried to joke, but she had tears in her eyes.

"Do you mind if we watch?" Patty poked her head around the partition where I had been getting ready.

"What?" I wasn't paying any attention.

"Can we watch you jump back in time?" Patty repeated.

"Yeah, I guess. It doesn't matter to me."

Patty clapped her hands with excitement, and Melanie gave her a shove.

Usually, when I time jump, I go in blind. Meaning I've never been to the location before. Tonight was different. I was going to picture the basement cellar and direct the universe to place me there, but sometimes it takes me a minute to regain my equilibrium when I time travel, and I didn't want to risk jumping into hand-to-hand combat.

Instead, I decided to focus on the women's restroom at Sal's. I pictured every detail I could remember, right down to the brass wall sconces and miniature rose wallpaper. Even if the space had been renovated in the decades since, the picture in my mind should be clear enough for the universe to get the general gist.

The last thing I saw before I was sucked into space was the look of shock on Patty's face. If she weren't obsessed with the Agency of Paranormal Particularities before, she would be now.

Finally, luck was on my side as the restroom came into focus. The image at first was faint and watery, waving in the distance. I squeezed my eyes shut to keep the dizziness at bay and focused on the destination.

But as I was spinning though the jungles of time and space, something went wrong. I suddenly felt like I was toppling head over heels like a somersault. The tumbles picked up in momentum, as if I were speeding downhill. I tried to throw my arms out to stop myself, but I had gained too much momentum. If I didn't stop soon, who knew what year I'd end up in.

"HELP!" I yelled, or it might have only been in my head. I couldn't tell you. Either way, I was in trouble. Nineteen twenty-seven must've been too far back for me to attempt solo.

My magic couldn't hold on to the spell. I tried to picture Michael in my head and direct my energy toward him, but it was hard to think clearly when my world was spinning out of control.

"I got you!" Agatha's voice rang in my head. My feline familiar's power mixed with mine, stabilizing the energy.

I suddenly felt wrapped in a warm embrace.

Everything slowed, and I was pulled back as if on a bungee cord. The years blurred back in reverse. Instead of being dropped with the Redcoats in colonial New York, I was back to facing the Roaring Twenties.

"Steady now," Agatha advised.

"I've got it now," I replied in my head. My eyes popped open when my feet hit the tile floor.

"Oh! Where did you come from?" An older woman with tightly curled gray hair and a sharp nose stared at me with wide eyes. She had been drying her hands when I materialized.

"I'm sorry. I didn't mean to startle you." Even though my stomach was still rolling, I reached out and touched the woman on her bare upper arm. I held my fingertips there for a moment. The woman gave a bit of a jump as if she had been shocked, and she probably had been. "I didn't realize the bathroom was occupied. My apologies. I'll wait outside until you're finished."

I removed my hand, and the lady blinked at me in the mirror's reflection. I smiled in return and slipped out the door.

As I made my way down the hall toward the kitchen, I quickly realized that it didn't matter what Veronica had said; my dress was completely out of place. The women I passed in the dining room had on longer dresses with scooped necks and capped sleeves. I couldn't have stood out more if I was dressed like a clown doing the hokey-pokey.

"What are you doing up here?" an older gentleman hissed in my ear.

I whipped around. The man before me was tall and slim, dressed in a business suit. "Entertainment uses the facilities downstairs." He glared at me and gripped me by the upper arm, pulling me quickly out of sight from the dining room and into the kitchen.

"Sorry, I forgot." I pulled my arm back.

"Jerry, they need you over at table two," another man in a suit called over to us.

Jerry nodded to indicate he'd heard the man before turning to me. "Just don't let it happen again."

"Promise." I quickly scooted away, weaving my way through the rest of the kitchen and back to the stairwell.

It wasn't until I was standing in front of the bookcase that I realized I didn't know what to say to gain entry. Luckily, I only had to wait a minute for someone to exit the club.

"What are you doing?" a burly man said once he took in my appearance. Now he was a shifter. I could tell just by looking at him. Shifters always made the best bouncers.

I was going to reply that I was there to dance or listen to some music, something witty, but my eyes were immediately drawn to the crowd. The place was packed. The air was hazy wit cigarette smoke. The din of the crowd spilled into the entryway. "Hurry up and get on stage. They're about to start." The man patted my backside, and I was about to turn around and zap him when I realized it was my perfect excuse to slip inside.

What I wasn't planning on was the woman who grabbed my hand, laughing and pulling me along with her. "You must be the new girl. Betty said you'd be starting tonight. I'm Alice, and we're up!"

"Wait! Wait!" I protested.

But Alice didn't wait. In less than fifteen seconds, I found myself standing front and center on the stage. Three other girls were already waiting for us. They smiled encouragingly, happy as a clam to have me join them. I realized we were all dressed about the same with loose sleeveless dresses and high heels. The girl standing in the center put her hands on her hips, turned to the band behind us, and gave a nod. The trumpet player signaled back, and loud, brassy notes instantly filled the air. The girls took their cues and started dancing the Charleston. I quickly tried to copy the steps and found myself wishing I would've paid more atten-tion in dance class when I was in second grade. I found myself flailing my arms back and forth, step-ping forward and backward, trying to copy the other girls.

I quickly realized that the men in the audience didn't really care what dance steps the girls were doing as long as beads were flying and legs were showing.

I kept my eyes on the cellar room door as it opened, and another shifter exited. This man was even bigger and burlier than the bouncer. They must be Merrick's henchmen. I quickly danced my way off the stage and into the shadows behind the stage's thick, velvety curtain to think. I needed to use my brain here. The quicker I could get in that room and rescue Michael and get out, the better.

"What's your plan?" I mumbled to myself, eying the space.

It was there, behind the stage, where the idea came to me. The exposed electrical box was nothing like I'd ever seen before, with the fuses looking more like shotgun shells than the modern switches I was familiar with. On the floor beside it was a case of empty bottles.

I knew what I had to do.

I didn't hesitate. I ran forward and with one hand grabbed an empty bottle. I put the other on one of the two main breakers, sending a power surge through the grid. Sparks flew into the air. The club was instantly plunged into darkness. The band ceased playing, and before anyone could come to investigate, I lowered my voice and yelled out, "Raid!" Then smashed the bottle on the ground.

With one simple word, everyone panicked. Chairs scraped across the floor, and ladies screamed. I stood behind the curtain, eyeing the cellar door. I could barely make out what was happening, but I heard the door pull open and the henchman came barreling out, asking what was going on, but it was too late. The club was in complete chaos. I snuck into the back room, realizing I hadn't factored in how hard it would be to navigate in the darkness. It wasn't empty like it was in 1964. The room was stacked with crates, which I could only assume were full of liquor.

"Michael!" I whisper-yelled with my hands out in front of my face to keep me from walking into things.

A faint grunt replied in the corner. I stumbled forward, hitting my knee on a low crate. I didn't feel the pain as I sidestepped the obstacle and felt my way in the dark.

"Michael?" I tried again.

Again, the grunting followed. I realized someone must've gagged Michael. If not, he would've been shouting to the high heavens.

I scrambled in the darkness, running into more things despite my best effort to avoid them. I soon found myself crouching on the ground in front of my boyfriend.

"Oh my gosh, you're alive. Thank you." I took his hands into my own. They were frozen like ice.

"Vee?" Michael's breath came out like a whisper. He wasn't gagged, but he was weak. The room was so dark, that I could barely make out his features.

"That's right. I'm here. Can you stand?"

Michael didn't reply, but I could feel him struggling to move. "My legs. They're not working right."

"Here, let me see." I put my hands on his knee and sent a little bit of my power into him. It was a low hum to try and get his blood flowing. "Is that helping?" I tried to keep the panic out of my voice, but I had no idea how much time we had until the henchman returned.

"I think so," Michael's voice was rough and scratchy.

I scooted myself closer and put my arm under his waist. Michael's whole body felt like ice. It seeped out of his clothes and into my skin, causing me to shudder. "Let's try to stand on three." I counted down and then hoisted Michael up. It was a team effort, and we used the corner of the wall as support to shuffle back until Michael was upright.

A loud crash came from outside the door, and someone shouted. "We have to get out of here."

Michael sagged against the wall. "I don't know if I can."

"You can and you will," I replied. *Even if I have to carry you up those stairs*, I thought.

Michael staggered forward. His weight leaned heavily on me.

"Just don't stop," I commanded, using the forward momentum to keep moving, hoping Newton's first law of motion was true.

Michael stumbled, his legs intertwined with mine, and we almost went down. A stack of crates toppled to the floor, but I didn't stop moving. I kept my power humming which was acting like a battery pack for Michael.

Chapter 16

If it weren't for the complete madhouse, Michael and I never would have been able to escape undetected. We limped along, weaving through the crowd. The club was trashed as people fled the scene. Climbing the stairs was the worst. Nothing but sheer willpower and the force of the crowd thundering behind us forced us to the top.

Once outside, the hot summer night air felt sticky on my skin, or maybe I was just sweating from fighting to get Michael out of the basement.

"We can't stop moving," I said to myself as much as to Michael. My chest heaved from the exertion. Michael's complexion looked sallow under the evening light. His eyes were sunken, and his lips were blue. If he wasn't walking, he'd look like a corpse.

Michael continued to lean heavily on me.

Everyone had filtered out through the side kitchen door, which spilled out into an alley. We trudged forward, looking for a cab while the rest of the patrons scattered into the night. Make that, I was looking for a cab. Michael's eyes were closed.

"Come on," I jostled my side and pulled him along. Michael's legs practically dragged. Who knew how much time we had until the shifters realized he was missing? If they found us now, we'd be toast. I could escape, but I wouldn't be able to take Michael with me. I could only pray it wouldn't come to that.

Thankfully, I knew where we were. The Brooklyn Bridge stood like a beacon in the distance. Michael's knees buckled. "Steady there," I replied, staggering with him. I needed to get him someplace where he could rest, fast.

I flagged down the first cab I saw.

"Is he all right?" the cab driver asked over his shoulder. He eyed Michael suspiciously as I propped him up against the back of the car so I could open the door. Once open, I pushed Michael down, unceremoniously plopping his backside on the bench seat, and then moved one leg into the car and then the other as if he were paralyzed. I'm sure it looked odd, but we didn't have any time to explain or even come up with a viable excuse. I couldn't even lie and say Michael had had too much to drink. With the sale of alcohol being illegal and all, it would only lead to more questions. "Bad clams," I improvised as I climbed in on the other side. "He's fine now," I quickly added before the driver could kick us out. Michael's head rolled to the side, leaning against the inside of the door. His eyes were once again closed. Can you take us to The Fitzgerald, please?" I took a five-dollar bill out of the front of my dress and passed it forward to the cab driver. His eyes widened with surprise, but he took the cash without another word.

If my adrenaline wasn't still pumping and I wasn't deeply concerned about Michael, I would've been able to admire the taxicab itself. I've come to realize I have a thing for cars. It's one of the things I enjoyed most about time travel—seeing how our means of transportation have evolved. The car puttered along. My eyes kept flicking over to Michael.

"Does he need a doctor?" The cab driver was back to being concerned.

"Oh, no. He'll be okay." I attempted to smile. The effect was half-hearted at best.

There were a couple of reasons why I chose The Fitzgerald. One was because I knew the agency's affiliation with the hotel, and two, I remembered reading in the hotel's brochure back in my room in 1964 that the luxury hotel was built in 1918 and boasted en suite bathrooms with bathtubs. A big deal for the time and something Michael was in dire need of to help warm him up.

I held Michael's hand the entire ride. Not so much as a means of affection, although that was a nice bonus, but more to keep a steady stream of my energy pulsing into him. I sandwiched his hand between both of mine, but his temperature never grew warm. Meanwhile, I felt like I was roasting with the constant energy I was generating, not to mention I was still recovering from the labor-intensive escape. I blew down into my cleavage, trying to cool myself off. It was a pointless attempt.

I squeezed Michael's hand as we drew closer to the hotel. He cracked open his eyes. The rest of his body remained unmoving. Michael looked dead to the world. I swallowed the uncomfortable ball in my throat. Visions of rescuing Michael and quickly jumping back home were quickly slipping away.

Michael and I shared a knowing look. I had a dozen questions to ask him, but I couldn't utter a single one, not where we were. Not that Michael was up for a lengthy conversation.

The cab rumbled up to the valet. I scooted out of the car and walked over to Michael's door. Thankfully, he didn't fall out when I opened it. It seemed to take every ounce of strength for him to hoist himself out of the car and stand tall. I gave Michael a moment to gain his balance. I was going to slip my arm around his waist to help keep his balance when Michael offered his arm to me. Together we trudged through the hotel's front door.

Michael still felt chilled to the bone. I felt his arm tremble as I held it. A hundred magical curses flew through my mind. I was going to spell Merrick into oblivion once I got my hands on him. He deserved no less.

I scanned the lobby for the closest chair as soon as we entered and spotted one about twenty feet up ahead. I steered Michael that way and helped ease him down.

"You know how to pick them," Michael tried to joke as he took in the grand lobby. His speech was slightly slurred as if he had just had a shot of Novocain from the dentist. "Sorry, that sounded funny," Michael remarked, picking up on the missed articulation. He smacked his lips. I had a feeling he couldn't feel them either.

"I'll be right back." I hated leaving Michael in a semi-frozen state, but it was better than having him pass out at the registration desk.

"Good evening, and welcome to The Fitzgerald. How may I be of service?" a gentleman behind the grand marble counter asked when I approached.

"Hello, my husband and I were wondering if you had a suite available, preferably on the first floor?" I motioned to Michael, thinking it was best to present as husband and wife. Michael tucked his hands under his thighs as if trying to warm them up. His teeth chattered.

"Is the gentleman alright?" The clerk craned his neck to get a better view.

"Fell off the pier. Afraid he's chilled to the bone." Again, I improvised. "I found him a change of clothes, but I fear he'll need a hot bath and a warm meal before feeling better."

"I see." The clerk seemed unsure, but he still looked down to consult the registration book. After a moment, he looked back up. "My apologies, but I only have a grand suite available on this floor." The clerk sounded grave.

"How much is that?" I kept my voice light and optimistic, hoping I had enough.

"Nine dollars." The clerk looked regretful.

I almost replied, *That's it?* But instead, I carefully schooled my features. I knew I had given the cab driver a decent tip, but I hadn't realized it had been that good.

The clerk didn't wait for me to reply before adding, "I have other rooms available."

"Oh, no. We'll take the suite."

"Are you sure? Would you like to talk it over with your husband first?" The clerk looked concerned. Bless his heart. He wasn't trying to be sexist. He seemed genuinely concerned that Michael would be upset if I booked the room.

"I'm positive." I didn't even look over at Michael, but I did turn around. Unfortunately, I hadn't thought ahead. Once again, I needed to fish the cash out of my bra. I retrieved the money as discreetly as possible, quickly removing a couple of bills. They turned out to be a twenty and a five. I handed the twenty over. I wasn't about to make change in my undergarments.

The clerk took the money and mumbled something I couldn't make out. I was convinced he wasn't sure what to make of me. I doubt whatever conclusion he drew was wholesome. Truthfully, I didn't care what he thought of me or my indiscretion. I'm sure he had to have witnessed far more scandalous behavior in the heart of New York City, even if this was the 1920s.

I then glanced back at Michael. He was shivering uncontrollably. "Can you hurry, please?"

Within a few moments, the clerk finalized the registration and handed me the key. I wasted no time going to Michael and helping him down the hall. Thankfully the room wasn't far at all.

"Okay, how are you feeling, and what can I do for you?" I said after I eased Michael onto the bed.

He sat on the edge, rocking back and forth. "I'm just so cold. Every muscle is clenching. I can't get warm." The words came out in staccato.

"Even with a healing spell?" Michael was a decent healer. Something his sister insisted upon once he became a police officer.

"Not working. My powers are frozen."

"Sit tight." I went and peered into the bathroom. I was relieved that the brochure hadn't lied. I'd never been happier to see a bathtub. "I'm going to draw you a bath. Give me a moment." I worked to do just that, making sure the water wasn't too hot or cold. A warm bath could feel scalding when you were numb from the cold.

"I've got it," Michael said after the bathtub was half full. With a Herculean effort, he lifted himself off the bed. I moved to assist, but Michael ignored my efforts. "I'm fine," he said, even though he moved at a snail's pace, shuffling his feet into the adjacent room. As grateful as I knew Michael was for my rescue, he was also a man who had his pride. The last thing he probably wanted help with was bathing. I understood that. I would be the same way. I just didn't want him to drown. Regardless, I hung back and gave Michael some privacy, which meant that I was left with a bunch of restless energy.

I paced the room, wondering how I could help. It quickly came to me. Food, I could get him some food. The Fitzgerald had a ground-floor restaurant and rooftop dining. I had no idea what the take-out situation was in the 1920s or if room service was an option. I remembered hearing a food vendor when we got out of the cab, which I suppose could always be an option. Unfortunately, it was late. I assumed the food carts would disappear any minute and I'd have to find change for the bills. I couldn't go out tossing cash around like I was made of money all night. I had a feeling we might be here for a couple of days. We might need it.

"I'm going to go see if I can find something for us to eat," I spoke over the running water. I couldn't exactly hear what Michael replied, but it sounded something like good.

As I made the short jaunt back to the front desk, I tried to think if I knew any warming spells. Michael was obviously under a magical attack. I had no idea if the effects would wear off on their own or if we would have to develop a counter spell. It was times like this when the Internet was handy. Nothing like a little research to solve your problems.

"Yes, Mrs. Cooper?" the front clerk said when I approached the counter once more. It turned out the man wasn't so put off by my behavior to be disrespectful. That, and appearing seemingly stuffed with cash didn't hurt either.

I relayed my question about dining options.

It turned out that the hotel was willing to provide a tray of hot tea and soup, seeing my husband wasn't feeling well. The hotel clerk saw to everything while I waited in the lobby. A kitchen staff member soon brought a tray out, complete with a teapot, two bowls of vegetable soup, and a loaf of bread. My stomach growled as I took control of the tray.

Back in the room, I tried not to fuss over Michael, but he was taking an awfully long bath.

"You okay in there?" I asked once again through the closed door.

"Still cold," Michael replied.

"I have hot tea and soup. Maybe that will help." I eyed the tray longingly. I had planned to wait for Michael before eating, but my stomach protested. I eyed a second chunk of bread. There was nothing better than real butter on warm, fresh-baked bread.

I heard the water slosh around while I was fantasizing about sourdough, followed by a loud SPLOOSH! I was off the bed, ready to jump up and save the day, when Michael hollered, "I'm all right! I slipped, but I'm out now." Shortly after, he came out of the bathroom, wrapped in one of the hotel's towels. Michael eased into bed, and I took the comforter and pulled it up around his waist to help keep him warm. Michael leaned back against the pillows and closed his eyes. "Before I forget to tell you, thank you," he said, still with his eyes shut.

I smiled softly. "You're welcome." I doubted Michael even heard the words. He appeared to be fast asleep. It looked like he'd have to eat later.

Chapter 17

The following day Michael's condition hadn't improved much. He managed to eat a bit of scrambled eggs and drink some tea, but he was still chilled. His magic refused to fire.

"I feel like I have the flu," he mumbled while huddled under the blankets, shaking.

"I'm sorry. I'm trying to figure out how to help."

I didn't want to sit around and wait to see if Michael got better or, heaven forbid, worse. And he was in no condition to time jump out of here. Even I wasn't powerful enough to jump us both back to 1964. I barely made it here, which probably had to do with the fact that it was almost a hundred-year time jump from where I was from.

Still, I had to act. I scrunched my brow in concentration. I knew where the magic shop was in the sixties, but I doubted it was there now. Radio

Alley was in its prime, and Chuck's didn't go into business until after radio declined. I tried to think of where else I could go. I needed someplace where I could research spells. Where could that be?

Then it hit me—the library.

I remembered Lester saying something about the New York Public Library having a special section. I wondered if it existed in the 1920s and if there would be a spell there for me to use.

There was only one way to find out.

"I'm running out," I said to Michael. I bent forward to feel his forehead. His skin felt cold and clammy. I frowned and stepped back, trying not to let the concern show on my face. "I'll be back as soon as I can."

"Mmmh-hm," Michael replied as he nodded off.

I gave Michael one last look and then headed out.

I couldn't walk around New York City dressed as a flapper during the daytime. I was used to being out of my element, but that didn't mean I wanted to look like it. Thankfully, New York City was iconic because it had existed much the same for decades. For example, I knew where Macy's was located, and they would have everything I needed.

It caught me by surprise how at home I felt in the city. After being a country girl for years, I could finally say I saw the appeal of the big city. Although, I must admit it was the New York of the sixties that felt the most like home and not the twenties. Even modern-day New York City was a bit much. The sixties were like a happy medium.

As much as New York was the same with the noise and the cars, it was also different. The skyline wasn't as tall. The billboards didn't flash and glow. And there were barely any streetlights. Police officers stood in the intersections directing traffic. The female officers wearing long pleated skirts and pill box hats, whistles perched between their lips. I hadn't given much thought to how traffic flowed through the city pre-city planning. In the distance, a man repeatedly yelled, "Hot dog! Hot dooooog!" from his vendor cart, and kids squealed as they splashed in spray from a partially opened fire hydrant. The car horns were different, but incessant, much like the steady thrumming of construction. Well, maybe that last part was the same.

I beelined it for the women's department and picked up the first frock that looked somewhat decent. Admittedly, the fashions of the day left something to be desired. Everything seemed to be collared and loose-fitting, with a strong preference for long sleeves even though it was summer. At least the material was light. I could now see why the flapper dress was so scandalous. I picked up fresh clothes for Michael and a beaded purse for myself, so I had somewhere appropriate to stash my money, and then checked out. I changed into my new dress in the fitting room, putting the flapper ensemble in the paper bag with Michael's new clothes.

My next stop was the library. Like a speakeasy, I was sure there was a special code or phrase I was supposed to use to access the special section. Of course, I had no idea what the words could be or where I should start to look. My plan was to use a spell to locate the area. I was basically going to use a spell to try and find a spell. That was before I realized how impressive the building was. I was gobsmacked. The library's main building looked more like a national museum than a library. I climbed up the steps, weaved between the three-story cement pillars, and pulled the massive door open. From there, I wandered aimlessly, letting my curiosity pull me around corners and up stairs. Soon I found myself standing in awe inside a capacious reading room with a multi-storied ceiling, arched windows, and cloud murals rivaling any grand cathedral. This room alone must've housed thousands of books. My task suddenly felt insurmountable.

I swallowed down the panic rising in my chest.

While summoning the book might be next to impossible, finding someone to help wasn't. Perhaps I could bewitch a librarian. I couldn't glamour people like vampires, but I could drop hints about what I was looking for, and if the librarian thought I was nuts, I could erase her memory. It was a weak plan, I knew that, but I wasn't sure what else to do. I didn't have time to search the entire library.

I placed my hands on my hips and exhaled, looking around for a librarian to approach. It would be better to find one off alone, restocking shelves, versus going up to the counter in front of witnesses. I stood off to the side, eying the aisles.

It was then, as I was standing there, that I smelled a very familiar and particular scent. I turned to the right and looked down the row of desks that filled the room. A young man sat hunched over a book. I casually sniffed his way and shook my head. Nope, the shifter scent wasn't coming from him.

I walked down to the next row and cautiously sniffed the air. The scent was stronger here. Out of the row, two desks were occupied. I walked behind the patrons. An older gentleman had a textbook in front of him, taking notes. The scent was stronger, but it still wasn't quite right. I walked past the older lady and stopped dead. The woman looked sweet as could be wearing a periwinkle sweater over an ankle-length dress. She had on white gloves and a pearl necklace. Her gloved finger trailed the text as she read along, her lips moving. I peered over her shoulder at the book's title. 101 Spells to Dispose of Your Enemies was scrolled across the top of the page in a fancy script.

I gently placed my hand on her shoulder. The

woman didn't even flinch as if she had known I was standing behind her. "Yes, dear. What do you need?"

"Sorry, I was just wondering if you could tell me where you picked up that volume?"

The woman turned and gave me her full attention. Her eagle eyes scanned my face. "I don't think I know you," she replied hesitantly.

"No, I'm from out of town, but I'm looking for a similar book to help one of my friends." We were speaking in code, and we both knew it.

"Very well, if you found me, you must be worthy of the password. Second floor, third door on your right. It looks like a broom closet. Tap on the wall three times and say hopscotch. The room will reveal itself."

"Thank you, I appreciate it." I nodded my thanks and turned to walk away.

"Good luck, dear," the old woman replied and went back to reading her book.

I repeated the directions as I climbed up the stairs. I needed to go to the second floor, then the third door on the right. Second floor, third door on the right.

I followed the directions to a T. I knocked three times inside the storage closet and said hopscotch to the blank wall. All par for the course in the world of magic.

Moments later, the wall seemingly dissolved

before me, and I stood in front of a quaint space. The room had several narrow-arched windows and five or six rows of books. It felt like I'd stepped into someone's private library.

An elderly man with a long white beard, wearing a blue velvet robe, poked his head out from behind one of the shelves. "Oh, hello. Welcome."

I stepped down the two steps onto the library's deep mahogany floor. The staff had arranged clusters of armchairs below the windows. Warm light poured in, giving the space a cozy feeling.

"What can I do for you, Miss?"

"This is a lovely space you have here."

"No place better if you ask me," the man agreed. He pushed his wire-rimmed spectacles back onto his nose.

"I'm grateful I found you. I have a problem. Maybe you can help me." I explained to the kind wizard, because surely that's what he was, what had happened to Michael. "I suspect it's a frozen spell of some kind, but I'm not sure which one or how to break it."

"Don't fret. I know just the thing."

"You do? Do you know what spell he's under?"

"Don't have to. All you need is a little bit of dragon whiskey. It'll warm him right up."

"Dragon whiskey?" I wasn't familiar with it.

"It's old-time magic, but it works."

"Do you know where to get it or how to make

it?" I winced at the thought of me mixing up a potion in the hotel bathroom. But desperate times called for desperate measures.

"Sure do. I know a guy. Here, let me get you the address. He owns a produce stand two blocks up the street. Just tell him Old Mickey sent you. He'll fix you right up. Good guy, I promise."

"Dragon whiskey, huh?"

"If that doesn't work, nothing will."

"I'll give it a try. Thanks for all your help."

The wizard wrote down the information.

"This place is pretty special." I marveled at the private library once more. I would have to bring Michael back when he was feeling better.

"Come back anytime. I'll be here," the wizard said as I left.

The visit to the library hadn't gone how I had expected. It had gone even better. I followed the wizard's directions and walked the two city blocks until I saw the produce stand on the corner.

Much like today, it seemed everything was sold by the quart or the pound, but the prices were much lower. Peaches were $0.17 a pound, and I wasn't sure about the tomatoes. An oversized number twenty-five was painted on a sign next to the bushels. I wasn't sure if that was $0.25 a bushel, a quart, or an individual fruit. The stand owner was finishing up with a customer, and I held back. I continued to look at the offerings and thought I should pick up a couple of apples and peaches to snack on. They did look fresh. I grabbed two of each, and as soon as the man wrapped up his conversation, he turned to face me.

I blinked a time or two. I couldn't believe who I was seeing. "Sid?" The man I knew as a newspaper stand owner in his seventies was now a much younger produce stand owner, and he was quite handsome.

"Yes, hello. Have we met?" Sid cocked his head. There was no way to explain how I knew him, so I quickly recovered and said, "Old Mickey sent me." I leaned forward. "I'm looking for some dragon whiskey?"

"I can do that. How much do you need?"

"Enough to cure a frozen spell?" I shrugged my shoulder, indicating I had no clue.

Sid nodded. "I have just what you need."

"Here, I'll take these also." I put the apples and peaches on the counter. Sid took out a brown bag, slipping a small bottle into it before adding the produce. The movement was so fluid that I would have missed it if I hadn't been watching. Everything rang up for less than a dollar. I shook my head. I was still having a hard time wrapping my head around the difference between the prices in this time period and the inflated prices I was used to.

"See you soon," Sid replied, tipping his newsboy

cap, which he'd still be a fan of in the sixties. I waved goodbye and headed on my way.

Michael looked the same when I came back. I'm not even sure he had moved in the two hours I'd been gone.

I sat on the edge of the bed and gently rubbed his shoulder. He groaned under my touch. "Hey, I have something for you to try," I softly spoke as he came to.

"What is it?" Michael mumbled.

"Dragon whiskey. A wizard told me about it."

Michael cracked open his eyes. I stood up and walked over to the bag, retrieved the bottle, and pulled out the cork stopper.

Michael scooted back and sat halfway up.

"A wizard?" Michael tried to raise his eyebrow in question, but his face must've been frozen because his brow only went halfway up.

"I'll explain once you're feeling better."

Michael lifted the bottle to his lips and tipped the contents back. He shut his eyes tight and swallowed it down.

"That good, huh?"

"It burns," Michael exhaled and shook his head. "It doesn't taste bad, but it feels like I'm swallowing fire."

"Maybe that's a good thing." I hoped that meant that it was working.

Michael leaned back against the pillows and closed his eyes. "I hope so."

"You hungry yet?"

Michael shook his head. "No, maybe some tea?" I stood up and checked the pot from this morning. It was barely lukewarm. I said as much.

"That'll work."

While Michael drank the tea, I filled him in on my afternoon.

"You ran into Sid?" Michael's voice sounded stronger.

"I know, crazy. Part of me wishes I could've told him I knew him from the future. I know he would've gotten a kick out of it." Sid was a regular human, but he knew all about the supernatural world. I never did know how, but I was grateful for his knowledge, especially if the dragon whiskey restored Michael's health. I looked over at Michael. He no longer looked so pale.

"I think I might take another bath." Michael pulled the covers back and stood up. He was still wearing the towel from last night.

"I bought you some new clothes too. I'll put them in the bathroom."

"Come here," Michael held his palm up.

I walked over and put my hand in his. He pulled me close in a tight embrace. I nuzzled my nose under his chin. Already, he was feeling warmer.

"Thank you," he replied over my head. I knew Michael was thanking me for more than the clothes.

"I just did what any magic-wielding girlfriend would do," I said to his chest.

"No, it's more than that. You're my world. I want to make sure you know that."

I stepped back and looked up into Michael's eyes. "I do."

Michael kissed me in the middle of my forehead.

I stepped back. "Now you go take that bath. I'm going to lay down." I hadn't slept the night before, keeping an eye on Michael. The lack of sleep was catching up with me. I could feel it in my bones. I was asleep before the bathtub was even full.

Chapter 18

I woke up as the sky was turning pink. I must've been well and truly exhausted if I had slept the past twelve hours. Light filtered in through the half-closed curtains. When I turned to check on Michael, I realized that he was awake and watching me.

I cleared my throat. "How are you feeling?"

"Much better. Almost normal, I'd say."

If there ever was a moment to have an emotional breakdown, this would probably be it. A range of emotions flooded through me. Relief and gratitude competed for attention. I felt them both in equal measure. Michael brushed a single tear that rolled down my cheek away with the pad of his thumb.

"I was never going to give up," I confessed. I scooted up into a sitting position and wiped my face with the back of my hand, unwilling to melt into a puddle. I could cry later. I'm sure I would cry later. But right now, Michael and I still had a case to solve. "What happened anyway? And why is there a dead shifter in your closet."

Michael looked taken back. He copied me and sat up. "Dead body? What are you talking about?"

"After I missed you in the alley, I went back to your apartment to see if you were there. When you weren't, I started searching for your address book. That's when I found the dead body."

"I didn't kill anyone. I have no idea. Are you sure it was a shifter?"

"Oh yeah. The stench was pretty bad."

"Huh. I had nothing to do with that." Michael shook his head in sync with the words.

"What about the missing women? I know you were looking for Celeste, but another witch named Rebecca is missing too. Her daughter is devastated. Were they with you?"

"I don't think so. I tracked Celeste to the shifters. That's why they came after me." Michael paused as if allowing the memories to play back. "The last thing I remember, we were in the alley. I realized I couldn't take them, so I tried to run." Again, Michael zoned out before continuing, "That's when Merrick appeared and hit me with a freezing spell. When I woke, I was in the cellar."

"So, where's Merrick's hideout, and where are these women?"

Michael thought. "Do you want to try to scry for them?"

"Do you think you're strong enough?" I didn't want to drain whatever strength Michael had regained.

"Oh, I'm strong enough," Michael said with a wicked grin. "You want me to show you?"

"Something tells me we're not talking about magic anymore."

"Oh, it will be magical, all right. They don't call it the great rite for nothing."

I shook my head but smiled, nonetheless.

"Is that a good smile?" Michael tucked a piece of hair behind my ear.

"Good smile? No, it's a great smile."

LATER THAT MORNING, we decided to scry for Celeste. I had a general idea of what she looked like from the case photo, but I wished we had something of Celeste's to strengthen the spell. Hopefully, the two of us would be strong enough to get a clear hit. Michael and I stood in front of the bathroom mirror and held hands, combining our power. The power flowed between us like a closed circuit. I closed my eyes and inhaled, drawing in Michael's energy, and exhaled, releasing my energy in turn. We stood there for a few moments, comfortable in each other's presence. It was odd how a simple spell performed together could bring me so much peace. I felt at home.

"Ready?" Michael whispered.

"Go for it." I kept my eyes closed and functioned as a backup power source for Michael.

It wasn't until after he recited the incantation and squeezed my hands shortly after that I opened my eyes. "Is it just me, or does the image look fuzzy?"

I turned to face the mirror. We were huddled shoulder to shoulder in front of the small bathroom vanity.

"No, it's not just you." I put my hands on the sink and peered closer into the mirror. The image was like an out-of-focus picture. I could see Celeste, but her expression looked blurry. I knew from experience there wasn't anything we could do to sharpen it.

"What do you suppose it means?"

I pushed off from the sink and stood upright. "It means Celeste isn't in 1924. This is how it looked when I scried for you." This was why Merrick was such a hard man to take down. He flew from decade to decade at a second's notice. No wonder no one had ever caught him. I sighed in frustration. "Do you think you're strong enough to time jump?"

"I thought I showed you how strong I was."

"Yeah, yeah. No bedroom eyes. I'm serious. I

just got you back. I don't need to lose you in no man's land. I needed Agatha's help to get here." Michael's brow furrowed in concern. "Don't worry. I think heading back will be easier. Especially together." I hoped so, anyway.

"I'm good. Promise," Michael confirmed.

"Okay, then I say we jump back to Sera's apartment. She lives in The Village."

"Sera Lexington?"

"I honestly don't know. She's a coven leader if that helps. Irene and the girls introduced us."

"Sera Lexington." Michael nodded. "And you saw Irene? How's Archie?"

"They're not together."

"Really?"

"I'll explain later. Your sister's at Sera's too." Michael started to ask another question. We still had so much we needed to discuss. "Let's time jump first, and then we'll talk."

"I was just going to say the same thing."

Chapter 19

"Michael!" Karen broke into sobs as the two of us appeared in Sera's living room. To the coven, it looked like I'd only been gone seconds.

"That was amazing!" Patty exclaimed. "Did you see that? Vee was there, and now she's here, and she found Michael!" Patty turned to Melanie and Irene. Even Melanie seemed impressed, seeing she didn't bite back with some witty retort.

Karen put her hands on Michael's face, cradling his cheeks and staring at her baby brother. "I thought we lost you." Karen didn't even try to stop the tears streaming down her face. "And Vee, thank you for bringing my brother home." She turned and wrapped me in a bear hug.

OOF! The air squeezed out of my lungs. Karen let me go, and I took a deep breath.

"Can I use your phone?" Karen asked Sera. "I

have to call home and tell them Michael's all right." Karen turned to Michael. "You are all right?"

Michael nodded.

"Be my guest," Sera pointed to the corner where her bedroom was.

My eyes glimpsed a figure in the opposite corner. The girl folded her arms across her chest. Her face tipped up toward the moon. I could only imagine the thoughts swirling in Abigail's head.

I looked back at Sera. "Michael was the only one there. We tried scrying for Celeste, but the image was out of focus."

"They're in a different year," Sera surmised.

"That's what I think. We could try to use Abigail's blood to track her mom, but we don't have a relative of Celeste's to do the same. I wish there was a way we could track Merrick." It was an impossible task. I didn't even know his last name, let alone next of kin.

I looked over at Michael. Sera was explaining the potion we had used to track him. Michael nodded, but something about his expression seemed off. He wasn't actually paying attention.

Michael looked away when I tried to catch his eye.

Uneasiness slid into my stomach. "What aren't you telling me," I interrupted Sera, keeping my voice low.

Sera looked taken back. She didn't know Michael's subtleties the way I did.

"Can you excuse us for a moment?" Michael didn't wait for Sera to reply. He took me by the hand and led me out the front door and into the hall. You would think the close contact brought me comfort, but it only added to my suspicion.

"I already know you were working for the agency. What I want to know is what else you're not telling me." I hadn't planned on having this conversation right that minute, but now wasn't the time for secrets.

"There's no easy way to tell you this, so I'm just going to say it. The reason the agency asked me to take the case and not you is because Merrick is your father. They didn't think it was right to assign you the case. They weren't sure how you'd react." Michael's eyes searched my face.

I swallowed uncomfortably as I tried to process my thoughts. "Merrick, is my father?" My voice sounded cold, detached.

Michael nodded.

"A dark warlock has kidnapped witches for who knows how many years, and he's my father?" My voice was a mixture of disbelief and disgust. "How is that possible? Is the agency sure?"

"They sounded sure."

The puzzle pieces began to click into place. "That's why Deacon said it was a conflict of interest," I said to myself. "He's the one that gave me your case file. But there wasn't anything in it about Merrick being related to me." That wasn't the type of information you glossed over.

Michael shrugged. "It wasn't in the case file. It was confidential. I don't even know if Deacon knows."

"Oh, I'm sure he knows. Wait until I get my hands on that little twerp." Anger began to pulse within me. All these years I'd been working for the agency, and they knew who my father was, and they never told me? "Didn't they think I might want a chance to take the man down?"

"I don't know. You'll have to ask them."

"Believe me, I will," I bit back. And then I thought of something, and I couldn't believe it. I remembered looking at the case file, and there was a picture of Merrick. The man looked to be in his mid-thirties. In other words, the same age as me. I brought it up to Michael. "How is that even possible?" As far as I knew, no one had created the philosopher's stone.

"I don't know. What do you say we track him down and find out?"

I ignored Michael's question. "Were you going to tell me?"

Michael raked his hand through his hair.

"Looks like I have my answer." I turned to walk away.

"Vee, wait. Yes, I was going to tell you, but I had no idea how. It's not something anyone wants to know."

"But I have a right to know."

"I agree. I'm sorry you found out this way."

"Me too." With that, I turned around and left Michael in the hallway.

———

I ASSUMED we were going to be time jumping somewhere in New York City. It was the location that made the most sense given Merrick's history. Imagine my surprise when the potion revealed that he was in Trenton, New Jersey during the same time as us.

"Trenton?" I looked to Michael.

"He's in Jersey?" Michael said at the same time.

"Are you sure?" I said to Sera. Her scrying spell was the one that pinpointed the location. The potion is what gave us the date.

"I'm one hundred percent confident."

Michael leaned over Sera's map. Her quartz crystal had landed with a decisive thud, scoring the map along the river front.

"Okay, I guess we're going to Jersey." I looked over to Michael to see if he was ready to go.

"You can't be serious. We can't take off right now."

"Why not?"

"Don't you think we should contact the agency and tell them we found him? We can get a team together and go in with backup."

"You mean the agency that's been lying to me my entire career?"

"Don't do that."

"Do what?"

"Get so angry you do something stupid."

I glared at Michael. "I could do without your tone," I bit back.

"We need backup, and if you take your emotion out of this, you will see that I'm right."

I didn't say a word. Truthfully, I knew Michael was right, but I didn't want to admit it.

Michael sighed. "I'm not trying to start a fight." Michael struggled to find the right words. "But, if you go in angry, you might make a mistake. I could never live with myself if something happened to you."

I understood where Michael was coming from, but didn't he want revenge? What if we waited too long and Merrick jumped out of here? What if the potion didn't work next time and we couldn't find him? I couldn't let the man get away. Not this time.

Michael lowered his voice. "Can we talk about this in a little bit?" I hadn't realized we had garnered a crowd, but every member of the coven with staring at us, slack-jawed. "Let's go back to my place, change, and come up with a plan. Okay?"

I nodded but didn't say another word. I was already one step ahead of Michael, my brain whirling with what we should do next.

Chapter 20

We said our goodbyes to Sera and the rest of the witches, promising to call them if we needed their help which we knew was a possibility. Karen left with us. She wasn't ready to let her brother out of her sight.

"I told Gran we'd be at your place if Sam calls to check in," Karen said from the back seat of Michael's car.

"Sam?" Michael asked.

"He was in town, looking for you," Karen remarked as if that was obvious.

"When's the last time you talked to him?" Michael kept his face forward but directed the question to his sister.

"Last night, why?"

Michael seemed to think before he spoke.

"Michael?" Karen said in the tone that only an older sister could master.

"I may be a bit worried, that's all. I wouldn't have brought him in if I had known how bad it would get."

"I'm not mad at you for that. Maybe for you not telling Vee what you were up to, but not for asking Sam for help."

I smiled from the front seat. Have I mentioned how much I adored Michael's sister?

When we got to Michael's, we walked into the apartment as Sam walked out. We all stopped for the briefest moment, a second suspended in time, before the two men closed the distance and clapped one another on the back.

Sam grabbed Michael by his shoulders. "Man, don't ever do that again." Sam was about the same height as Michael; only his coloring was lighter with sandy blond hair and blue eyes.

"Don't intend to." Michael cleared his throat.

"I was just leaving you a note," Sam turned to me. "I figured you might be staying here again. I wanted to give you a heads-up." Sam looked unsure.

I had a feeling I knew what he was talking about, but the foyer wasn't the place to have this conversation.

"How about we take this inside?" Michael suggested. He took the words right out of my mouth.

As soon as Michael closed the door, I said, "This is about the dead shifter, isn't it?"

"Dead shifter? What dead shifter?" Karen began to search the apartment with her eyes. "Are you telling me there's a dead body here? Did you kill someone?" Karen's voice ratcheted up a notch.

"I didn't kill anyone," Michael replied.

"You didn't?" This time it was Sam.

"No. Vee already asked me."

"I thought maybe in a struggle," Sam mumbled.

"It must've happened after I left," Michael surmised.

"Hang on, how do you know about the dead body?" I turned to Sam, who was staring at a spot on the floor.

He snapped his head up. "I might have been the one to hide it. But he's not here now. I thought maybe the two of you disposed of it."

Karen looked between her husband and Michael and then me and Michael with disbelief. "Can someone tell me what is going on?"

I took the lead. "Someone killed a shifter in Michael's apartment. It wasn't Michael or me. Your husband came over and found the dead body and hid it. Then, when I showed up, I found it. The agency's cleanup crew took care of the rest."

"Ah," Sam nodded. "Would be nice to have one of those on the force."

"The agency might be hiring." Maybe he could have my job. I was still boiling mad at my employer.

"No." Karen vehemently shook her head. "It's bad enough you fight crime in Philly. I don't need to worry about someone kidnapping you to another time."

I nodded, conceding Karen's point. She and Sam had a beautiful family. He couldn't be jumping back in time at the drop of a hat, risking life and limb.

"Who killed the shifter then?" Sam asked.

No one said anything, but I had my suspicions. Call it more of a hunch. That was the least of our problems, and I said as much. "I'm not worried about the shifter right now. What I want to talk about is our plan to take down Merrick."

"You found him?" It was Sam again.

I continued doing the talking, "He's in Jersey. We have the general area, and I'm sure we can take him down together." I refused to look at Karen.

"The four of us?" Karen spoke up and demanded my attention anyway.

"You'd be more of a decoy," I replied, unsure if that made her feel better or worse about the plan I'd thought up on the way back. "Merrick has to know Michael's escaped by now. If my suspicions are right, he's going to hunt him down." I turned my attention to Michael. "He knows you're on to him, and if I know anything about psychopaths, they don't like to lose." No one said anything, so I pressed on. "I say we make a show of going out to dinner and being out and about town, having fun. Infuriate the man. Let him know he can't beat us."

"We go on with our lives like we don't care about him," Michael followed my train of thought.

"Exactly. There's a reason why Merrick has escaped capture for so long. He eliminates everyone who comes after him. The hunter becomes the hunted. Now that you're on his radar, he won't stop coming for you until you're eliminated." I wasn't trying to be dramatic. It was the truth.

"We need to kill him first." I was shocked by Karen's statement. I thought for sure she'd balk at the plan, but she had a fire in her eyes that most likely matched my own. I hated Merrick for who he was. Karen hated him for what he'd done to her brother. Together, we would make sure that he paid.

"Right. So, let's let him think we have our guard down," I added.

"It's a good plan, but we still need more than us. I don't want to rely on our fists," Michael added.

"I have an idea about that too. There's a spell book that might help." I thought of the book the older shifter woman was reading at the library. The title offered one hundred and one ways to rid yourself of your enemy, and we only needed one. "Do you know about the special section at the library?"

"Yes, why?" Michael looked hesitant.

"We're going to kick it old-school and set up a trap," I replied with a winning smile.

"And use Michael as bait. I like it," Sam remarked. His sister swatted him with the back of her hand in the middle of his chest.

"Hey, if you're going to smack anyone, smack Vee. It was her idea." Sam rubbed his chest.

"No one's smacking anyone. We don't have time for it. Let's head to the library and see what we can find." It was time to take down an evil warlock.

"HEY, MICKEY. HOW'S IT GOING?" Michael said as we entered the secret library. We left Karen and Sam at Michael's so they could call and check in with the family.

The old wizard looked up from behind the circulation checkout desk. "Michael! How have you been?" The wizard then took in my appearance behind Michael's shoulder. "Well, I'll be. If it's not the Miss who needed dragon whiskey."

The wizard's comment left me speechless for more than one reason. One that he remembered who I was. From his point of view, it was forty years since I had stopped in, and it was only for that one visit. And two, the old man looked exactly the same. I couldn't keep my curiosity at bay. "How is it that you remember me, and you haven't aged a day?"

"I could claim to be a time traveler like yourself," the old man chuckled. "But the answer isn't anything quite so adventurous." The wizard motioned to the books. "This entire room is filled with magic. Stay in here long enough, and it seeps into you."

"Fascinating. Can you leave?" I was just full of questions.

"I do, every day. But I always come back," the wizard winked. "Now, enough about me. What can I help you with today?"

"I'm looking for a book."

"Well then, you've come to the right place."

I went on to describe my plan. I needed a spell, something to catch Merrick off guard and stop him in his tracks. I needed to dispose of my enemy, so to speak.

Mickey was thoughtful for a moment. He stood there, stroking his beard, looking up at the domed ceiling. "What you need is a magical grenade."

"I beg your pardon?" Surely, I hadn't heard him correctly.

Michael was more familiar with the term. "A grenade might work."

"What's a magical grenade?" Perhaps I had been relying on my lock picking skills and ability to manipulate electricity for too long.

"With grenades, you create a portable spell. Usually, it's a potion," Michael began to explain. I gave an inward groan. Again, with the potions. Michael was going to have to help if we were going to get these grenades to work. I didn't trust myself mixing up anything more than a cocktail.

"You pour the potion into glass bottles. When you need to use it, you smash it on the ground and release the spell," Michael finished explaining.

"But you must say the intended's name." Mickey pointed his finger at me. "That's very important. If not, the spell will attack anyone."

"Good to know," I said under my breath.

Mickey began to move around the library. Michael and I waited for the wizard to find the book he was looking for and bring it back. I read the title: Portable Potions for Witches on the Go. Mickey handed the book over. "It's best if you use light bulbs. They're quick to fill and easy to break."

"Lightbulbs, got it," I remarked, accepting the book. Step one of the plan was complete.

Chapter 21

Later that night, our plan was in place. I felt like an evil genius when we made the reservation at Sal's Fine Dining. It felt almost fitting that we were going to celebrate at the club that had held Michael prisoner. You couldn't be more blasé than that. We were stacked to the brim with light bulbs too. I had four in my purse, as did Karen, plus more in the car. After dinner, the plan was for Michael to appear to walk by himself to fetch the car while I waited for him. Anyone who was watching would think that Sam and Karen had already left for the night when in reality, Karen was keeping watch from the car, and Sam and I were taking up our positions in the alleyway, ready to jump to Michael's defense.

Some people get nervous going into battle, but I was excited, ready to take Merrick down. It didn't hurt that I was confident in my abilities. I knew I was a powerful witch. Sam, Michael, and Karen could also hold their own. I had all the faith in the world in my team.

Michael walked out the front door of Sal's, whistling a tune. We purposely made our dinner reservations late. That way, the streets were almost empty. Michael couldn't have made it more tempting if he had held a neon sign that said, 'Kidnap me!' You'd have to be a fool not to jump at the opportunity.

Sam and I crouched behind the metal trash cans, waiting in anticipation.

"Hey, where you going?" A gruff voice came from behind Michael.

I turned to Sam and smiled. Shifter, I mouthed.

Sam nodded, telling me he picked up on the scent too.

"I'm getting my car. What's it to you?" Michael turned and squared his shoulders at the would-be attackers.

"Our boss man's not too happy with you. Heard you ran out on him."

Michael backed into the alleyway where Sam and I hid. "Well, if Merrick doesn't like it, tell him to come here and talk to me."

Michael was now twenty feet in front of us. We could see the two men closing in. If they had a lick of common sense, they would realize Michael wouldn't be walking backward down an alley if he was truly on his own.

But shifters aren't necessarily the brightest supernaturals in the bunch, especially when they were the hired muscle.

"That's not how this works. Haven't you learned that yet?" one of the shifters said.

"Yeah, we're going to rough you up and take you to him."

"I don't think so. Not tonight," Michael replied nonchalantly. "You tell Merrick to meet me here."

At that moment, the first shifter turned and whistled a high-pitched calling card in the nighttime air. Within moments, three more shifters appeared in the alleyway. I was hoping Merrick would join them, but it looked like we were going to have to take out the trash first.

The shifters made their first move, rushing forward to grab at Michael. But Michael didn't even need to use a magical grenade. He grabbed the shifter by the wrist and shocked him much the same way I would. The man yelped and jumped back. Sam and I then made our presence known. Together we chucked the light bulbs into the alley while Michael ran toward us, taking cover behind the trash can. The glass exploded. A swirl of red smoke billowed into the passage. Thank heavens, the wind was on our side and blew the smoke into the shifters' faces and away from us, seeing we didn't know their names to call out with the spell. Karen, a much better witch in the kitchen, had whipped up fire and freezing grenades. The fire ones didn't actually create fire but only made you think you were on fire. It was all an illusion. One that worked spectacularly even if Merrick didn't appear. It was still satisfying to send the shifters responsible for kidnapping Michael howling off into the night. The best part was that I still had my frozen magical grenades at the ready for future attacks.

Karen waited for the smoke to clear, and then she greeted us at the front of the alley. "You guys, that was amazing. I've never seen anything like it. You okay?"

Our trio walked toward Karen. "Yeah, I'm fine. You guys?" I turned to Michael and Sam. They both nodded that they were.

"That was almost too easy," Sam remarked.

"Too bad Merrick didn't show," Michael sounded frustrated. I didn't blame him. We might have to rethink our plan. I had assumed Merrick would do the dirty work himself, but I suppose I should've known better. "Maybe he'll be frustrated enough now to come after you himself."

"You're right. Maybe I will." I stood in shock as Merrick appeared inches away from Karen. He gripped her from the back of the neck and smiled an evil grin. "Let the games begin." Before he could time jump and disappear, I lunged forward and latched onto Karen's arm, and together we were sucked into Merrick's spell.

MY HEELS CLICKED on the concrete when we landed. I let go of Karen and stumbled backward, unable to gain my balance from the quick jump. Something told me we had just changed location, and not the year since we were in the middle of a factory. Oversized chrome vats marched down the space in a row. The cylinders reminded me of something you'd see at a dairy farm. The entire room was bathed in a blue glow from the moonlight filtering in from the windows above and reflecting off the chrome. More manufacturing equipment took up the space. A conveyor belt serpentined through the center of the factory.

I ran and hid around the corner, instigating a dangerous game of cat and mouse.

"Vee? Where did you go, my darling," Merrick called out. His voice echoed in the space. I swallowed and looked to either side of me. Unsure of which way to go, I darted to the left. My hands rested on the cylinder in front of me. I tried to gain my bearings and come up with a plan.

"Let me go," Karen demanded. They were not more than twenty feet away.

"I don't think so," Merrick growled.

As I stood there figuring out what to do next, my eyes had a chance to adjust to the darkness. To my horror, I realized the front of the vat wasn't chrome but glass, and it was filled with clear liquid. Worse, a woman was frozen inside.

I gasped and jumped back, crashing into a stack of boxes. One of the boxes fell on top of me. Thankfully, it wasn't heavy. I kicked the box off and was ready to run, but not before the logo caught my eye. It was the Jolly Time Ice Cream Stamp. We were in an ice cream factory. You had to be kidding me. What type of psychopath froze people and made ice cream? And what did that say about me if I shared his gene pool?

Then it all started to make sense--why Merrick was kidnapping witches and why he looked so young. He was freezing the witches and siphoning their power, which meant the women weren't dead. They were under a spell. The relief I felt was brief. I still had to take Merrick down and not meet the same fate as these women.

Merrick struggled to pull Karen along as he hunted me down.

"Quit struggling," Merrick commanded. I spied them through the industrial equipment. Karen, one to always think on her feet, fell back until Merrick had to pull her along. Once behind him, she kicked him in the back of the knee, causing his leg to buckle, and then twisted out of his grasp and ran away.

Merrick cursed and turned to chase her when I stepped out from hiding. "Leave her alone. She's not that powerful, and isn't that what you want? Us powerful witches?"

"Ah, there you are. I was wondering why you were hiding. Welcome home." Merrick clapped his hands in delight. "What do you think of the place?"

I bit back my scathing retort. Merrick was clearly unhinged. I quickly realized I had to play my part right. "Home?" I tried to sound intrigued and not disgusted.

"You are, after all, my daughter."

"You know?"

"Of course, I know. I've been watching you for some time. You don't have to have the same fate as your mother. You can join me. It will be brilliant. I'll teach you everything I know. Absolute power will be at your fingertips." Merrick marveled at his power.

My throat worked hard at the mention of my mother. I couldn't hide my thoughts. "You killed her, didn't you?"

"Come now, do I look like a monster? You mother is perfectly safe right here. Vat number one.

She was, after all, my first." Merrick looked lovingly down at the end of the row.

The earth rolled under my feet, and I fought to stay upright. If what Merrick was saying was true, then my mother wasn't dead, but under a spell. My heart hammered, and my power fought to unleash. I wanted to grab Merrick around the neck and send a thousand volts into his worthless body. I didn't care if he was my father or not. He didn't deserve mercy. The only thing holding me back was common sense. I couldn't forget who I was dealing with. Michael's words of caution floated into my consciousness, and I fought to control my emotions. There was no way I'd ever join forces with Merrick, but he didn't need to know that. "I don't know what to say. It's all so much." That part was true.

"I'm sure you'll see how brilliant my plan is. Once you're away from that pathetic man you think you love, you'll realize I'm a genius."

More like a madman, I thought.

"He'll have to be killed. I can't help it. Surely you understand."

I couldn't respond. I couldn't believe how nonchalant Merrick was acting about killing Michael. "Every time I try to kill him, he comes back. But you know what they say, never send a shifter to do a warlock's job."

"It was you. You killed the shifter in Michael's apartment."

"Not me personally, but one of my men. Just another one of their mistakes. They can't even kill the right person. Killed one of their own. Idiots." Merrick smirked.

I held my tongue, not that I knew what to say.

And then Merrick made a fatal mistake. He stepped into my personal space. "Think about it, my child. I see so much of myself in your eyes." Merrick put his fingertips on my chin and turned my head to look at me from a different angle. I don't know what he was thinking. Maybe he thought I was under his spell, but the moment his fingers touched my skin, I didn't hold back. My power erupted with a fury. My hand reached up and latched onto his wrist like a snake bite. I sent every volt of electricity I could summon into his body.

Merrick managed to let go. "You little--"

He never got the last word out. Before he could finish the sentence, I grabbed the magical grenade from my purse and smashed it on the ground. "Merrick!" I shouted. Blue smoke swirled around the dark warlock, freezing him in an instant. His body grew rigid, and ice moved up his body, encasing him in place.

"How about a taste of your own magic?" I shot back to his statue-like form.

Merrick stared back at me, unable to move.

"You were phenomenal," Karen appeared from behind me.

"Thanks." My eyes never left Merrick. I wasn't taking any chances.

"AHHHHH!!!!!" Sam materialized in the middle of the factory, holding onto Michael, and charged toward us. His own magical grenade held high in the air.

Karen and I turned and looked at him. It was sort of a where-did-you-come-from look.

Sam quickly took in the scene and lowered his weapon. "You took care of him? Nice. Although, I'd like to chuck a spell or two at his head. Are you okay?" Sam turned his focus to his wife.

"I'd say I'm impressed, but I never doubted you," Michael said, taking in the scene.

"Oh yes you did. I think we need backup," I lovingly imitated my boyfriend.

"It's never a bad idea to play it safe," Michael quipped.

Sam continued to check over Karen and make sure she was alright.

"How'd you find us?" I asked.

"Took a chance. Jumped to the industrial park. Your magical signature did the rest."

"You tracked me."

Michael nodded and then took in his surroundings. "All the missing witches," he said in wonder.

My throat grew tight. "Including my mother." I took Michael by the hand and led him over to the first glass cylinder. My mother floated in the magical liquid inside, looking exactly as I remembered her, right down to the shoes. "Do you think?" My voice choked, and I was unable to finish my question.

Michael knew what I was going to ask. "I think we'll do whatever we can to bring her back."

Chapter 22

"I owe you an apology," Director Standsburg said to me. As director of the agency, I knew who the man was, but I'd never met him personally.

Dozens of field techs and agents had descended onto the scene. No one was taking any chances. Merrick was too dangerous for one agent to escort into custody. While agents handled the transport, the techs were coming up with a plan to thaw the witches. "I never would've kept the information from you if I thought you could help. I only thought it would cause you pain. I see now that I underestimated you. It won't happen again."

I felt like responding with a dozen different replies. None of them were professional. In the end, I decided that the only person I could be mad at was Merrick. He was the man to blame, not

Director Standsburg and certainly not Michael. I understood that now.

"Thank you, sir," I replied before turning and walking away. I'm sure the director had more he wanted to say, but I wasn't up for it. My stomach was tied in knots, and I felt like I would be sick. I had searched for my mother for years, and now I'd found her. It was my biggest dream and nightmare come true.

Around us, techs debated the various potions and thawing spell options, but no one seemed to know what to try first.

"Do you think dragon whiskey would work?" I asked Michael.

"It unfroze me," he replied.

I turned and ran back over to the director. He was talking with another higher-up.

"Sir, about the counter spell, I know something that might work."

The agency tried to get me to leave while they freed the two dozen witches frozen in their chambers, but I refused. It didn't take long for the agency to locate dragon whiskey. I watched with bated breath as they used the liquid to restore Celeste and Rebecca. The women coughed and sputtered as they came to, but they had only been frozen for a matter of days. My mother had been under for years. I didn't want to watch in case it didn't work, shattering my heart into a million different pieces, yet I couldn't look away.

I was planning to hang back. Michael's arms were wrapped around me, holding me close. But the minute she was free and laid down on the gurney, I rushed forward. My mother looked timeless. Her blonde hair was styled much the same as my own. Her makeup was still as fresh as the day she'd jumped back in time.

The techs immediately covered her in a thick wool blanket except for her arm.

"May I?" I asked the tech.

"Of course."

I hesitated before reaching out and taking my mother's hand in my own. It felt frozen to the touch. Tears pricked my eyes. "I'm sorry it took so long. I didn't know where to look. I tried, Mama. I tried." The tears fell in earnest.

Michael appeared at my side and rubbed my back. I glanced back at him before looking back at my mother once more.

"We're going to try the dragon whiskey," the tech informed me.

I nodded, unable to speak. I squeezed my mother's hand as the tech started an IV and administered the potion. I tried not to count the seconds, but it was either that or go crazy waiting for some sign of life, any sign of life.

When I got to thirty, I thought all was lost.

But when I reached number forty-two, my mother fluttered her eyes open, and I swear my heart stopped. The air left my lungs in a WHOOSH. I couldn't speak. I could only look down at her in disbelief. Was this a dream? Was my mother awake? Tears of happiness replaced the tears of grief from moments before.

My mother blinked and then turned and looked at me, "Vee?" Her voice was a mere whisper.

"It's me, Mama. Welcome home." I squeezed her hand and then brought it up to my lips and kissed her knuckles. Joy spread through me. For the first time in forever, I felt whole.

Stephanie Damore Complete Works
Mystic Inn Mysteries
<u>Witchy Reservations</u>
<u>Eerie Check In</u>
<u>Spooked Solid</u>
<u>Untimely Departure</u>
Midnight at Mystic Inn
Bewitched Break Inn

SPIRITED SWEETS MYSTERIES
<u>Bittersweet Betrayal</u>
<u>Decadent Demise</u>
<u>Red Velvet Revenge</u>
<u>Sugared Suspect</u>
Indulgent Injury

. . .

WITCH IN TIME
Better Witch Next Time
Play for Time
Time Will Tell

BEAUTY SECRETS SERIES
Makeup & Murder
Kiss & Makeup
Eyeliner & Alibis
Pedicures & Prejudice
Beauty & Bloodshed
Charm & Deception

A DROP DEAD *Famous Cozy Mystery*
Mourning After

About the Author

Stephanie Damore is a USA Today bestselling mystery author with a soft spot for magic and romance, too. She loves being on the beach, has a strong affinity for the color pink (especially in diamonds and champagne), and, not to brag, but chocolate and her are in a pretty serious relationship.

Her books are fun and fearless, and feature smart and sassy sleuths. If you love books with a dash of romance and twist of whodunit, you're going to love her work!

For information on new releases and fun giveaways, visit her Facebook group at https://www.facebook.com/stephdamoreauthor/

facebook.com/stephdamoreauthor

twitter.com/stephdamore

instagram.com/steph_damore_author

bookbub.com/profile/stephanie-damore